P9-BJI-058

Guns Blaze on Spiderweb Range

Also by Walt Coburn
in Large Print:

Branded
Coffin Ranch
Law Rides the Range
Secret of Crutcher's Cabin
The Square Shooter
Violent Maverick

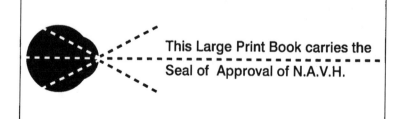

This Large Print Book carries the
Seal of Approval of N.A.V.H.

Guns Blaze on Spiderweb Range

WALT COBURN

Thorndike Press • Waterville, Maine

Published in 2002 by arrangement with Golden West Literary
Agency.

Thorndike Press Large Print Paperback Series.

The tree indicium is a trademark of Thorndike Press.

The text of this Large Print edition is unabridged.
Other aspects of the book may vary from the original edition.

Set in 16 pt. Plantin.

Printed in the United States on permanent paper.

Library of Congress Cataloging-in-Publication Data

Coburn, Walt, 1889–1971.
     Guns blaze on Spiderweb Range / Walt Coburn.
         p.   cm.
     ISBN 0-7862-4334-1 (lg. print : sc : alk. paper)
     1. Large type books. 2. Montana — Fiction. 3. Ranch
life — Fiction. I. Title.
PS3505.O153 G87 2002
     813′.54—dc21   2002021489

Guns Blaze on Spiderweb Range

I

The weekly arrival of the stage at Sundown was a gala event. The citizenry got dressed to the nines. Nester cowmen brought their families in to get the mail and to stay for the Saturday night dance. Cowhands drew their wages and came in to celebrate. The General Mercantile, the barber shop and saddle shop, and the saloons did a thriving business. Tinhorn gamblers broke out new decks. The women of easy virtue preened their sordid feathers.

A couple of cowhands from Cass McCandless' big Spiderweb outfit were tossing silver dollars at a crack on the wide plank sidewalk in front of the Lone Star Saloon. The six-horse stage was due around six o'clock in the evening. It was near that hour now. Both men kept watching the skyline for the dust cloud that would announce the coming of the stage.

One of the cowhands was a big, heavy-shouldered man with a shock of curly hair the color of new rope, and a badly set broken nose. Curly Mapes was a bronc rider who rode the Spiderweb rough string. The other cowhand was short and wiry, with a weasel-eyed face and a thin-lipped, cruel mouth. He packed a switch-blade knife and knew how to use it. Skeeter Owens was said to be the best brand artist with a running iron in any man's cow country. Both men drew fighting wages and earned it.

When Lorne Mackin, ramrod for the Spiderweb, rode into town with Curly Mapes and Skeeter Owens along with a couple more hand-picked hands who drew gunmen's pay, their coming put a blight on the gaiety. The Spiderweb had a tough rep. The men who worked for the outfit were Texans who had come up the trail with McCandless from his ranch in the Pan-handle, near Tascosa. It was the toughest trail town for its size between the Cana-dian line and the Texas border.

Big, gray-haired Cass McCandless was tough as a boot. He'd pointed his first trail herd north to Montana about fifteen years ago. He had turned three thousand head of Texas longhorns loose in early May. When he gathered them in September on the fall roundup, he claimed all the land they had grazed over and backed his claim with his gunfighters. If any of the small ranchers, whom he called scissorbill nesters, refused to sell out at his price, they were shot down or run out of Montana Territory. He had money enough to settle the damages and get away with it — and enough Tascosa cowhands to back his play.

His Spiderweb brand was a notorious cattle rustler's brand. Skeeter Owens could take a running iron and work almost any cattle brand into the Spiderweb. For some reason, Cass McCandless had managed to get the Spiderweb brand registered with the Montana Stockgrowers' Association. Once it was in the Association brand book, there it stayed, despite the efforts of the honest cattlemen to have it canceled.

The same was true of his ruthless land-grabbing steal. Every section of land in his vast empire was recorded in his name at the State Land Office. He gloried in the unsavory title of a ruthless cattle baron.

A year ago Cass had married a show girl from the Floradora chorus in a Chicago theater. Her name was Alison. She had almond-shaped, emerald green eyes, ash-blonde hair and an hour-glass figure and was young enough to be his daughter.

Alison McCandless, standing now in front of the plate glass window in the hotel lobby, stared out into the distance where the lowering sun turned the dusty stage road into a wide yellow ribbon. A brooding look shadowed her eyes. There was a bitter twist to her mouth that thinned her crimson lips. Her sleek hair, combed back in a severe line and bunched into a silken-webbed snood at the base of her neck, gave her features a clean-cut, cameo appearance. There was a cold aloofness to the young wife of Cass McCandless, a hidden fire beneath the lacquered veneer, as consuming and destructive as dry ice.

Sighting the distant dust cloud, she smiled inwardly as she turned to look at the two Spiderweb cowhands across the street. The hulking Curly Mapes stood on spread legs, his eyes squinted watching the approaching stage. He stood like that for a long time. Then hitching up his sagging cartridge belt with its holstered gun, he walked toward the swinging half-doors of the saloon.

Looking over them, he called inside. "She's a-comin', Lorne." Like some big men, Curly Mapes had a high-keyed, thin voice.

Lorne Mackin stood six feet two in his sock feet. The three-inch heels of his fancy shop-made boots added stature to his height. Wide-shouldered and lean-flanked, he dressed like a range dude in a red flannel shirt and tight-fitting, gambler-striped black pants shoved into his boot tops. His black Stetson, creased down the middle, Texas style, he wore at a rakish angle. He was a handsome man in a black-haired, swarthy, hawk-beaked, dangerous way. His Colt .45 was pearl-handled, silver mounted, the carved holster tied down low on his thigh with a whang leather string. As he shouldered through the door, the big rowels of his silver-mounted spurs jangled with each swaggering step.

Skeeter Owens picked up the two silver dollars with his left hand. Spinning one coin in the air, he slid out his six-shooter and shot it in mid-air. The dollar spun crazily and before it landed in the street, Skeeter flipped the second coin and shot it the same way.

There was a thin smile on his lipless mouth and a coldness in his pale eyes, as he cut a look at the hulking Curly. Owens ejected the two smoking brass cartridges and slid loaded shells into the chambers and replaced his gun in its holster before the last flat gunshot echo was gone.

Lorne Mackin was aware of the jealous rivalry between the two men, but he did nothing about it.

"You two mosey over to the post office. Be inside when the stage pulls in. You both got your orders," Mackin told them.

The Spiderweb ramrod crossed the wide street and stepped up on the plank walk in front of the hotel. With his hand he wiped the dust from his clothes and polished alligator boots. His eyes glinted strangely as he looked through the window at Alison McCandless.

As they stared at one another through the glass partition, a dark, angry flush crept into Mackin's swarthy skin. His eyes burned hotly as his stare stripped her as naked as she had been in the can-can line. He had first seen her like that when he'd sat with McCandless in the bald-headed row in a Chicago theater. As if she were reading his obscene thoughts, Alison's lips moved soundlessly. There was no mistaking the vile name he read in the movement of her scarlet lips.

With something gone from his arrogant swagger, Lorne turned away and walked back across the street. He shoved through the half-doors and took his place at the end of the bar. He splashed whisky into a shot glass and drank it down, refilling the glass a couple of times before he got the

bitter taste out of his mouth. He was downing his fourth drink when the stage rolled to a stop in front of the post office.

"On time to the second, Miz McCandless," the desk clerk said, grinning fatuously. "We set our clocks Saturday when Hank Sanford balls the stage in at Sundown. Could be that's how the town got its name. Sundown, Montana." He giggled at his stock joke.

If Alison heard the pompous little celluloid-collared clerk in the red necktie, she gave no sign. Her green eyes were staring at the six-foot, handsome man sitting beside the grizzled stage driver. The man was in his late twenties. His sunburned face looked as if it had been hewn from dark red stone by a dull chisel and a heavy mallet. His hair under the gray Stetson was the color of darkened copper wire. The Stetson and black boots marked him for a cowpuncher. The tailored suit pegged him as having lived in a city. Whatever the driver said made the young man laugh, showing a set of strong white teeth.

Alison narrowed her eyes ever so slightly. Some secret thought quickened her pulse to put a trace of color in her cheeks. There was the ghost of an enigmatic smile on her red mouth. She walked to the door with

13

the effortless grace of a professional dancer and stepped outside. On the boardwalk, she stood motionless and poised.

"End of the line, Doc," the stage driver said, as he tossed the mail sacks from the deep leather boot under the seat.

The stage passenger stepped down. There was a trace of quiet humor in the man's voice as he looked up from under the slanted brim of his hat. "Hand me down Solomon and his tribe, Hank."

From the roof of the coach the stage driver slid a box about the size of an apple crate. Two sides of the container were covered with chicken wire. Gently he handed it down to the man on the boardwalk. "Old Sol's got more wives and kids than a Jack Mormon prophet. Take good care of 'em, Doc."

The man pulled a battered suitcase, a bedroll and a sacked saddle from inside the empty stage. "That I'll do, Hank, and much obliged for fetching me up to date on everything," he said, as he thumbed back his hat.

Hank touched his hatbrim, and kicking off the brake, he cracked the long whiplash over the heads of the lead team and took off in a cloud of dust toward the livery stable.

Jim Benton, Veterinarian, stood there, his booted feet set apart as if he were bracing himself for some ordeal. From under his hat brim his eyes swept back and forth along the street as though he might be expecting someone to show up to greet him. His sunbleached brows were knit in a puzzled frown. For a moment there was a worried expression in his eyes. Then he shrugged it off.

Felix Carruthers, the skinny, crotchety postmaster of Sundown, came out for the mail sacks. As notary public and mayor, undertaker and coroner, and Justice of the Peace, Felix Carruthers was an important citizen of Sundown. And if necessary, he could preach a funeral or even baptize babies.

Jim Benton, grinning, reached out to pick up the two bulky sacks of mail to lend assistance to the sickly-looking postmaster.

"Hands off!" The words exploded like a .22 pistol. Jim Benton dropped the sacks. "Those mail sacks are the property of the United States Government!" Carruthers declared in his best courtroom manner.

"Sorry, mister," Jim Benton said, backing away. "I was just trying to lend you a hand."

The postmaster was reading the label on

the crate. "U.S. Department of Agriculture," he said aloud. "Dr. Eben Barnes, U.S. Experimental Station, Grasshopper Creek, via Sundown, Montana." He glared at Jim Benton through watery eyes. "What's in it?" he snapped waspishly.

"King Solomon and his wives and offspring," Jim said, poker-faced.

"How's that again?"

"Guinea pigs," Jim Benton explained. "Pigs is pigs. You keep Solomon and his tribe a week and you'll learn the hard way."

Jim Benton turned his head at the sound of a woman's laugh across the street. He stared, a little off balance, at the tall blonde girl in the dark green riding habit. He kept on staring. Alison McCandless had that effect on most men. Jim Benton, lifting his hat, grinned back at her. Then she turned and went back into the hotel. Jim went into the post office and stood at the general delivery window for his mail. Turning around, he watched Curly Mapes and the wizened Skeeter Owens arm themselves on either side of the door to the street. He met their stare with a faint, humorless smile.

If these two were a sample of the tough Spiderweb cowhands the stage driver had told him about, Jim Benton had a good chance to size them up for what they were. Carefully he looked them over from hat to boots, and his grin twitched slightly to one side of his wide mouth.

"What's on your mind, young feller?" The postmaster's voice startled him.

"Mail," Jim Benton said through the metal grille. "Benton. Jim Benton."

Felix Carruthers took the letters from the B pigeonhole. "James Benton, D.V.M.," he read. "That you, mister?" Like a card player, he held the letters fanwise in his left hand. "What's the D.V.M. stand for?" he asked, suspiciously.

"Doctor of Veterinary Medicine," Jim Benton replied.

"You headed for the Quarantine Station where they got the sick cattle impounded?"

"That's right."

"Then you might as well take this mail pouch along." He handed over a small mail sack. "That old fossil at the station hasn't been in town for ten days."

"You mean Dr. Barnes?"

"That's the man. Some kinda professor. Loco as a sheepherder, if you ask me."

"Nobody's asking you." Jim shoved his three letters into the inside pocket of his coat.

17

"Come to think about it, the old coot's afoot out there. The two half-breed helpers he has handling the cattle and dipping vat came to town with his mule team and old army ambulance a few days back. Got on a drunk and haven't sobered up yet. I saw the team and ambulance at the barn at noon."

From the corner of his eye Jim Benton saw the curly-haired man move away from the door and the other one close it and lean against the door. The one with curly hair stood behind Jim Benton, the man's breath fanning the back of Jim's neck. "Let's have the Spiderweb's mail, Baldy." He shouldered Jim Benton to one side. "Quit takin' up so damn much room, Dude."

Jim Benton, seeing the swing coming, sidestepped to duck the blow. If it had landed, it would have torn off his head. Instead he caught it on the shoulder and saw the glint of a set of brass knuckles on the huge fist. Before Curly Mapes could get his balance, Jim's right fist sank deep into the man's belly. Curly's breath gushed out with a whistling sound and the gun in his hand slid away. Jim smashed a right to the face as Curly went down, snapping the nose bone. Blood spattered. Then Jim kicked at his teeth as he hit the floor.

Skeeter Owens waded in, and Jim felt the whetted point of his switch-blade knife as it slashed across his belly, ripping his flannel shirt. His fist slammed into Skeeter's leathery face. Pain shot into Jim's arm as he bruised his knuckles on the bared teeth. As Skeeter's head snapped back, he choked on a mouthful of broken teeth. Jim Benton kicked his boot into the little man's guts.

Jim Benton backed away from the two men on the floor. He never saw the man standing in the doorway with a gun in his hand. As the barrel of Lorne Mackin's gun chopped down, the inside of Jim's head exploded. His knees hinged and he went down like a sledged beef.

Dizziness and nausea held Jim Benton pinned to the plank floor of the post office. Pain hammered inside his head. The meaningless jumble of voices made a humming sound in the black whirlpool of his brain. There was the taste of blood in his mouth where he'd been booted in the face.

He lay motionless as the words separated, taking on meaning.

"Get out of here!" That was the bald-headed postmaster's whiny voice. "You got what you came for. Now get the hell out of town, Mackin. Take these two jaspers and get going."

"Tuck in your shirttail, Baldy." Mackin's voice was toneless and ugly sounding. Jim Benton felt swift-moving hands go over him.

"That red-muzzled feller you knocked in the head is a government man, Mackin," creaked the postmaster. "You sure cut the big gut if you've killed him. Clear out and take this pair of hoodlums with you."

As they left, Jim Benton opened a cautious eye. He got a good look at Lorne Mackin. Then he rolled over onto his hands and knees and slowly stood up. He picked up his hat and slapped the dust from it, denting it in four places. A trickle of blood oozed from a three-inch scalp rip and the knife scratch had left a thin line of blood across his belly.

"I did what I could," Carruthers said from behind the wicket. "But my duty was to defend the mail, first, last and always, so I kept the door locked."

"I'll take the mail pouch for the Quarantine Station now," said Jim Benton.

The bald man stared at him. "You got the mail pouch," he cackled.

"If I had it, I wouldn't be asking for it."

"I shoved it under the grating before I gave out the Spiderweb mail. When the ruckus started, I slammed the window shut."

There was no trace of either mail pouch. Jim Benton felt for the letters he'd put in the inside pocket of his coat. The letters were gone.

A small crowd had gathered outside the post office. Somebody had opened the end door of the crate and let the guinea pigs out. A boy about fourteen was scrambling around trying to pick them up. His freckled face was flushed, as he put the pigs he caught into his old Stetson hat. His thick, straw-colored hair was matted with sweat. A broad grin showed buck teeth.

A girl about eighteen, in faded denim Levi's and boots and a blue flannel shirt, guarded the crate. Her tanned face was flushed, her hazel eyes alive with excitement. Two thick black braids hung down below her waist.

Lorne Mackin and four of the Spiderweb cowhands, Curly and Skeeter among them, rode down the wide street at a slow lope, their hands on their guns. When they had ridden out of sight, men, women and children came from doorways and began to mill around the post office, mumbling.

Jim Benton took a handkerchief from his pocket and wiped the blood from his bruised mouth and stared at the be-speckled postmaster with cold suspicion.

"I swear to gawd, I had no hand in it," he whined.

"You're accusing yourself, mister."

"Easy, Speck," Hank Sanford, the grizzled stage driver, said to the boy. "Old Sol and his tribe are worth more than a car-load of Texas longhorns."

Hank turned his head as Jim Benton came up behind him. "One of them Spider-web cowhands opened the crate, Doc," Hank explained. When he saw the knife-ripped shirt, his smile died.

"You got off lucky, Doc," said Hank.

"I found out the hard way." He nodded toward the freckle-faced kid and the girl. "Who are they?"

"Matt Wagner's young 'uns. Matt adopted the freckled kid when he was a yearlin'. Terry's his own daughter. She runs his hoss outfit. Matt's blind." Hank lowered his voice to a whisper. "Matt Wagner is one man who wouldn't sell out to Cass McCandless. Him and old Chiz McDougal, his neighbor, made a stand against the Spiderweb gunslingers. Both of them got shot up some. Old Chiz walks

22

with a limp and Matt's got a bullet lodged against his backbone. The doctors claim it can't be gouged out without killing him.

"Speck," Hank said to the boy, "shake hands with Doc Benton. He'll want to thank you for rounding up Old Sol and his tribe."

The boy's slate-blue eyes looked straight into those of the man as they shook hands.

"I owe you something, feller," said Jim with a grin.

"I got paid off," Speck said, soberly, "when I saw the job you did on Curly Mapes and Skeeter Owens. Too bad you let Lorne Mackin get away."

The girl got to her feet, flinging her head back defiantly.

"Meet Doc Benton, Terry," Hank cut in quickly. "This is Terry Wagner I was telling you about, Doc."

Jim felt the grip of the girl's fingers and the rough calluses in the palm of her tanned hand. A grin crinkled the corners of her eyes.

"Hank sure gave you a build-up, Terry. And I believed every word of it." Jim noticed the color mount to her tanned cheeks as she slid her hand free. Her eyes looked around, searching the crowd. "Where did Speck go to? I've got to find him."

"He ducked into the saddle shop, Terry," Hank called after her as she turned and ran up the street. Then he turned to Jim. "The team of government mules and the ambulance Doctor Barnes uses is at the White Elephant barn. I'll help you hook up, Doc."

When they had hooked up the mules to the ambulance, Jim Benton climbed into the seat and took the lines. Hank told him he'd be at the post office to load the crate of pigs when he drove past.

"How's chances to hire out, Doc?" It was the freckled kid speaking. He had come from somewhere inside the big barn. He stood hipshot like an old cowhand and tried to make his voice sound like a man's. "Those half-breeds quit the Quarantine Station. I'm old enough to make a hand."

"Pile in, feller," Jim Benton said.

"I got a horse hid out in the brush," Speck said. "I'll be at the big gate when you get there." He vanished as suddenly as he had come.

For a moment Jim Benton's eyes were bleak. Hank had told him about young Speck, whose real name was Chisholm Carver. His father had been killed and he had been brought to the Wagner ranch and raised by Terry's mother. Ever since her death, Speck had been running away.

Jim pulled up at the post office and Hank loaded the crate. He handed Jim a Winchester 30-30 carbine in a saddle scabbard and a couple boxes of cartridges. Then Hank loaded Jim's suitcase and sacked saddle.

"It's about fifteen miles to the Quarantine Station on Grasshopper. It'll be dark inside an hour, but there'll be a moon. Sure hate to see you pull out alone."

"I've been taking my own part since I was fifteen, Hank. I'll manage."

The sound of shod hoofs turned both men around. Terry Wagner reined her horse up beside the mule team. Her eyes were shadowed with worry. "Speck's coyoted on me, Hank. His horse is gone from the barn."

"Speck's hired out to me, Terry," Jim Benton told her. "I'll take care of him, so don't worry."

Jim Benton saw the troubled look leave the girl's eyes as she held out her gloved hand and gripped his tightly. There was something disturbing in her eyes as she looked at him, and he felt the blood pulse in his throat. Her gloved hand tightened in his and the warmth of her eyes were steady, without a trace of coquetry. He was uncomfortably aware that the crowd must be staring at them, holding hands for such a long time.

Terry Wagner must have sensed the same thing. The color that had flooded her cheeks ebbed as swiftly as it had come. But instead of jerking her hand away, she moved closer to him.

"I hate this town." Her whispered voice fanned her breath against his face. "The gossipy females look down their noses at me because I wear pants." She fought back the tears. "I'll give these females something to talk about!" Her voice was a shrill whisper. Without warning, she threw her arms around Jim Benton and kissed him on the mouth.

Pulling away from her, he said, calmly, "Easy, Terry," and then told Hank to tie her horse with the hackamore to the hame ring of one of the mules. Terry would ride with him part of the way home.

Jim Benton lifted her bodily from her horse and placed her on the seat beside him. When Hank had tied her horse to one of the mules, Jim kicked off the brake, and slapping the lines, the mules broke into a fast trot.

As Jim Benton leaned out sideways to wave farewell to Hank Sanford, he caught a brief glimpse of Alison McCandless standing behind the plate glass window of the hotel. There was a pale anger on her face and a curling twist to her mouth. In her clenched hands, she held the draw-strings of a mail pouch. Which pouch, Benton wondered.

"I could hug you for what you did back there," Terry laughed shakily, and put the words into action.

"That's the first time I ever kissed a man in my life, Jim," she admitted a little defiantly.

"You got nothing on me. That's the first time a girl ever kissed me, the way you did."

A strange silence fell over them as they rode along. Then Terry's laughter eased the tension and they began to talk. Once the ice thawed, they told each other things that each had kept hidden too long.

Terry reached for the sack of tobacco and papers in Jim Benton's shirt pocket. She rolled a cigarette and put it in the corner of her mouth, lighting it from a kitchen match. She pulled the smoke in and let it drift from her nose. Then she rolled another one into shape. "Want me to lick it, Jim?"

He nodded. He had never before seen a

girl smoke, let alone roll her own. But he kept that knowledge to himself.

"I rolled and smoked my first cigarette when I was fourteen. It made me sick as a poisoned pup. I didn't smoke again till I was eighteen. I'll be twenty next month," she added.

"You look about eighteen now," he said, trying to make it sound off-hand while he mentally calculated the seven years' difference in their ages.

"Tell me about you, Jim."

His eyes looked out into the gathering shadows of approaching nightfall, as he told her about his father and how he had hoped to become a doctor of medicine. "I had to work my way. Four years of pre-med at the University. I had to take it in three."

"Better that than nothing," she said softly.

"I didn't go to McGill University in Canada where my dad got his degree. Instead I spent two years studying to be a vet. I turned out to be a horse doctor. Right now I'm working out a system of checking what's called Texas Tick Fever in cattle that resembles Spotted Fever in human beings. It takes time and money."

"Why is Cass McCandless so bitter

against the experiment at the Quarantine Station? He's done a lot of speechmaking at the Stockgrowers' meetings and when the Legislature is in session."

Jim Benton smiled grimly. "If the State Quarantine goes into effect, as the result of the research work being done at the Experimental Station on Grasshopper and other places, Cass McCandless will be stopped from fetching any more cattle from Texas to Montana."

"A few hundred Spiderweb longhorns were fenced in under quarantine about a month ago. Perhaps whoever culled out those ticky cattle had some agreement with Cass McCandless." Terry made it sound like a question.

"The cowhands who did the job took their orders from the Stockgrowers' Association. Uncle Sam and the State of Montana are backing the Association, regardless of protests by McCandless." There was a quiet finality in Jim Benton's voice.

"The last man to take over the station," Terry said, "saddled his horse last week and rode away. He never came back. Either he sold out to McCandless or he was run off by Mackin — or bushwhacked on his way to Sundown."

Jim Benton added, "The man preceding him was dragged to death when he rode to town to get the mail. He had the mail and a town bottle, compliments of the Lone Star Saloon, when he left Sundown. He was riding a gentle horse. His body was mangled, but the pint of whisky in his chaps' pocket was unbroken."

"Then you know what you're up against, Jim."

"The man before that was dry-gulched. Shot in the back on his way from town." The faint grin on Jim's mouth was mirthless.

"Why didn't the Association or Uncle Sam do something about it?" Terry questioned.

"These things have to be handled with kid gloves, Terry. Cass' shyster lawyers could file suit for false arrest if he were charged with murder. He has the money to win."

"That's something," Terry exclaimed, "when a man like Cass McCandless can spit in Uncle Sam's eye." Her eyes were angry.

"You must have been listening to Hank Sanford. Only he put it in more forceful words."

"I can do that, too," Terry assured him.

Her eyes darkened. "So Uncle Sam sent you out to be murdered."

"Nope. I volunteered for the job."

"Why?"

"Several reasons," he said quietly. "Let's not go into it."

"Name one," Terry said sharply. "Just one reason why you sat yourself as a sitting duck for Mackin's gun-toters."

"I watched my father die of Rocky Mountain Spotted Fever," Jim said. "There's a definite tie-in with the so-called Texas Tick Fever in cattle and Spotted Fever in humans. I want to find it."

"I don't understand, Jim."

"There's a Dr. Roscoe Spencer, one of the best medical research men in the United States, who is devoting his knowledge and risking his life in a woodshed laboratory near Hamilton, Montana. He won't quit till he has discovered a preventive vaccine."

"They said my mother died of Rocky Mountain Fever. She got it from drinking melted snow water," Terry said.

"That theory is wrong, Terry. Typhoid, maybe, but definitely not Spotted Fever. I spent some weeks as one of Spenny's assistants. I studied bacteriology under Dr. Barnes, now at Grasshopper Creek. They make a good team, Spenny and Barnes."

"You mean that mild little man with the gray chin whiskers? I've met him a few times in town. Always looks like he's slept in his clothes," she said. "He looks at you through horn-rimmed specs without actually seeing you. Once I helped him load some boxes into this old ambulance and he said 'Thank you, young man.' I had my braids under my hat."

"Barney forgets to eat sometimes. He sleeps on a cot in his lab. I've worked with him in the lab twenty-four hours at a stretch. When I heard he was at the Grasshopper Station, I put my name in for transfer here."

"You knew what you were getting into, Jim?" Terry asked.

"Not when I sent in my application to the Department of Agriculture. It was when I attended a closed session of the Stockgrowers' Association that I was brought up to date on Cass McCandless and his Spiderweb killings. They laid it on the line."

"So the fly walked into the Spiderweb."

"Make it a horse fly."

"A yellow-jacket wasp." Her smile trembled a little. "At the fork of the road there ahead we part company. When we stop, put on your stinger." She picked up Jim's six-shooter from its shoulder holster and put it on the seat beside him.

When they reached the turn, he said, "I'd better drive you home, Terry. It's late."

"No, thanks, Jim. I always ride home alone."

Jim felt the blood hammering in his throat as he looked into Terry's eyes. Her lips were slightly parted. The next moment she was in his arms, her lips against his.

"I'm afraid for you, Jim," she whispered. "You're going into danger."

"I can take my own part. Speck said he'd meet me at the gate. I'll send him home. I don't want him to get hurt."

"You'd be wasting your breath. He likes you, Jim, and he can take care of himself. I'm grateful to you for hiring him." Terry looked searchingly into his eyes and leaned over to kiss him again. "I'd better go," she said quietly.

It was five miles to Grasshopper Creek from the fork of the wagon road.

An eight-strand barbed-wire fence stretched out for miles to close in the five sections of government land. When Jim Benton reached the pole gate blocking the road, Speck rode up out of the moonlight. The gate was wide open.

"Somebody shot the padlock off, Doc," Speck told him. "And they've cut every cross pasture fence and mixed all the cattle up." His voice was high-pitched with excitement. The short-barreled Winchester was across his saddle. A filled cartridge belt and holstered six-shooter sagged across his slim flanks. In the faint moonlight he looked like an old man.

"Ride behind the rig, feller." Jim Benton slid his Winchester from the scabbard and slapped the lines across the mules' backs.

Ahead he saw the empty feed lots, the big corrals and the long chute connecting the pole corrals. And in the dimness he located the long dipping vat and the board catwalk on either side. The whiteness of the two-story frame building and the outbuildings looked ghostly in the moonlight. Among all the buildings only one blob of light showed. It came from the unwashed window of the lean-to shed. Jim Benton headed the mule team for that lone light.

He reined up in front of the door and read the sign:

LABORATORY
ENTER AT YOUR OWN RISK

34

No sound came from within. Jim Benton kicked on his brake, wrapped the lines around the whipstock and jumped down. "Stay here, feller," he told Speck.

A tight core of fear centered within him as he pulled the whang leather latchstring and shoved open the door. For a few seconds he stood there, blinking his eyes into focus. Labeled bottles of all sizes lined the shelves. Under the window half a dozen Bunsen burners together with retorts of all sizes and descriptions were lined up on a long table. Rows of filled and labeled test tubes, and pestles, occupied the remaining table space.

Two high-legged stools were placed in front of the acid-stained table. In one corner of the room a flat-topped potbellied stove stood in a sandbox. The light, which Jim had seen, came from the Rochester lamp hanging from the ceiling. Beyond an unpainted clapboard partition was dim, shadowy darkness from which came a faint moaning.

Jim Benton crossed the plank floor in long strides. Behind the partition a man lay on an army cot under a blanket. On a low bench beside the cot was a loose-leaf notebook and a bottle of ink and pen-holders. There was a half-filled bucket of water with a long-handled dipper.

When he sat down on the bench, his hand trembled as he pulled down the blanket from a gaunt face with a week's stubble of white whiskers. Thinning wisps of white hair lay dankly on the sweat-covered skin, the color and texture of old parchment. The eyes behind the bifocal lenses were sunken in dark purple sockets. There was a blue-gray line around the mouth.

The man's pale skin was hot to Jim Benton's touch. Gently he pulled away the blanket and saw the blotched, black-spotted skin on the man's naked body.

Dr. Barnes was dying from the deadly Rocky Mountain Spotted Fever. A poignant ache twisted Jim Benton's heart as countless memories of his father flooded back. He forced himself to return to the laboratory.

Speck stood in the doorway, his gun in his hand.

"Dr. Barnes," Jim said quietly, "is in there dying from Spotted Fever. For all we know the Spiderweb gunmen are hiding out in the barn or somewhere around the place."

"No, Doc," Speck assured him. "I hid out and watched them ride away. I got a good count on them."

"Then put up the mule team and your horse."

"You want the guinea pigs fetched in here, Doc?"

Jim Benton nodded. One glance at the notebook told Jim Benton that the stricken man had kept an hourly record of the symptoms of the fatal disease. He had left a thick letter, sealed and stamped, addressed to Dr. Roscoe Spencer, Hamilton, Montana. The letter was marked *Personal* and *Special Delivery.*

Jim went back behind the partition. His hands were gentle and a little unsteady as he removed the glasses and with a clean damp towel, he wiped the sick man's head and face. Dr. Barnes was in the final stages of the disease. There was nothing Jim could do except to sit there and watch the elderly man die. He put the thermometer between the blue lips, checked the uneven pulse beat, and recorded it.

The dying man's eyelids blinked and his fever-bright eyes fixed on Jim's face. "Jim . . . Hugh Benton's boy . . ." The words came faintly. "God must have sent you . . . no man likes to die alone. . . ."

Jim held the dipper of water to the man's lips and let him sip it. "Listen closely," the doctor said. "There is positive proof — the Rocky Mountain Spotted Fever — caused by cattle ticks — the notebook — detailed hourly reports — of symptoms — written down."

"I found the notebook," Jim told him. "I'll mail the letter to Dr. Spencer."

"Stout lad. Read Spenny's letter — mail it — with notebook — record pulse — check temp — every hour — until I die — color — texture blotches — scrape sores — put each on separate slide — mark slide with number — record in notebook — my watch —" His hands groped over the bench.

The watch had fallen to the floor. Jim Benton picked it up and read the inscription inside the case: Eben Barnes, M.D. Ph.D. from Fellow Colleagues of McGill University, Montreal, Canada. In Token of Love and Appreciation. Jim's eyes misted as he rewound the watch and sat on the bench to sit out the deathwatch.

After a long while, he folded the thin arms and pulled the old army blanket slowly up over the dead man's head. He turned the lamp on low and stood outside in the shadow of the lean-to, a mist filming his eyes.

Speck sat on the ground, his back to a

giant old cottonwood, with his carbine across his knees. His restless eyes moved from building to building, but they always came back to the shirtsleeved man who stood with bowed head, hat in hand, like a man deep in prayer.

But there was no prayer in Jim Benton's heart. Grief and a strange sort of bitterness tightened into a core of hardness. And after a time he straightened his bent shoulders and put on his hat.

There were certain things that had to be done: A grave to be dug, a pine box to be made, the dead shrouded. Jim had read the dying man's scrawled instructions to be buried on the little hill, for Dr. Barnes was a humble man.

"Reckon you could rustle up some boards, feller?" Jim asked Speck. "A hammer and nails, while I dig the grave?"

Speck looked up at the tall man. "You musta thought a lot of him, Doctor Jim."

Jim Benton gripped Speck's shoulder. "They don't come often . . . men like Doctor Eben Barnes. I was one of his students at Medical School. Some day I'll tell you about him."

While Speck nailed the sawed pine boards together, Jim dug the grave on the top of the little hill overlooking Grasshopper Creek. Together they buried him. And together, Jim Benton and the boy went back down the hill, side by side, sharing a silence that somehow drew them together in closer bondage.

II

Many things had to be done. The wires in the cross-pasture fence had to be repaired and the mixed cattle cut out and separated into their original feed lots.

Since Jim Benton had no horse, he saddled up one of the mules, and he and Speck rode into the big pasture. As they rounded up the longhorns in various stages of Texas Tick Fever, Jim pointed to the numbers stamped in white paint on their hides, explaining the method used in the slow, tedious job of tick eradication.

Each steer had to be dipped, then branded with a white number and the number recorded in what Jim termed the logbook. After two weeks, the cattle were dipped a second time until each critter had dipped a half-dozen times at two-week intervals. When the last of the cattle were tick free, they were turned loose into a clean pasture that had been idle for perhaps a year.

Jim Benton told Speck that when the female tick gorged itself on cattle, it dropped off and crawled under dead leaves or some shelter to lay thousands of tiny eggs. The seed ticks from the hatched eggs crawled up the tall grass into the brush and when a grazing cowbrute brushed past, the tick fastened itself to the animal.

It took them the better part of the entire day to cut out the cattle and drive each separate bunch into numbered pens after the cross fence was repaired and the cut wire spliced.

They finished working the cattle about sunset. While Speck cooked supper, Jim Benton broke the seal and read Dr. Barnes' detailed letter to Dr. Spencer. The opening sentence sent a chill into his guts: "This evening while I was undressing, I discovered a cattle tick fastened to my thigh. It must have been there since early morning because its belly was swollen from gorging my blood. I let it stay until it dropped off. I put it in a test tube and sealed and labeled it, and I made my first entry of the date and exact hour in my notebook.

"If your theory that the fatal Rocky Mountain Spotted Fever is caused by the cattle tick fastening itself to the flesh of a human being is correct, then I have per-haps contracted the disease. If so, I should within twelve to twenty-four hours produce symptoms that will either prove or disprove your theory. Perhaps if I had discovered the insect earlier I would have removed it, but I was too intent on the experiment of perfecting a cattle dip solution."

On a separate page under the heading S.B. (*Self Boiled*) was the itemized formula for arsenic stock dip. The rest of the page was devoted to specific directions for mixing the dip. The chemicals were to be stirred and heated to the boiling point, preferably in a five-gallon iron kettle or metal pan, not zinc or tin.

Jim Benton laid the sheet aside and resumed reading the letter written in installments on the hour. The last notation hit him a blow: "I can now definitely state that I have contracted Rocky Mountain Spotted Fever. This is the seventh day since the first symptoms appeared. I have kept hourly notes as to the progress of the disease since the first day the tick attached itself to my person. But from now on I will probably be unable to keep a complete hourly record. There is some dizziness that is impairing my vision, some nausea and periods of delirium."

Jim Benton put the letter into the envelope and went over to the frame house where he and Speck had made themselves comfortable. He fastened on his cartridge belt weighted down by the short-barreled Colt .45 in a worn holster.

"You want me to take the letter to Sundown and mail it, Doctor Jim?" Speck asked.

"Don't mail it at the post office. I don't trust Carruthers. Give the letter to Hank Sanford when there's no one around to see you."

"I'll be back before daylight," the boy promised.

Jim stood in the doorway of the stable and watched Speck ride off into the night. Then he headed for the lean-to where he had left Dr. Barnes' notebook on the workbench.

He started writing a duplicate of the recorded notes of Dr. Barnes so that he could send the original notebook to Dr. Spencer. In a few minutes he was so absorbed in his work that he failed to hear any outside noise. His back was toward the door as he sat on a high stool, bent over at his task.

The protesting creak of unoiled hinges brought Jim Benton upright and onto his feet. He was reaching for his gun when the sound of a woman's mocking laugh came from outside the opened door.

"You'd be a sitting duck, mister," the woman's throaty voice said, "for a bushwhacker. I'm Alison McCandless and I came here alone, to return the mail pouch you lost."

Jim Benton stood uncertainly for a minute before he said, "Come in."

"Enter at your own risk," she said defiantly. "Quite appropriate for the wife of Cass McCandless, but I prefer to remain outside in the darkness. There's always a chance of my having been followed."

Jim closed both notebooks and shoved them into a drawer. Putting out the lamp, he went outside. Alison McCandless stood almost within arm's reach. She was dressed in the same green riding habit she had worn when he saw her in town. Hatless now, her blonde hair took on a silver sheen in the moonlight and Jim could smell the musk perfume she used.

"Here's the mail pouch. Your letters are inside."

As he reached for the pouch, her hand closed over his. "Leave the pouch inside and come with me. I want to be near my horse, just in case."

Jim Benton tossed the pouch inside and then followed her past the corrals and dipping vat to her horse, a grain-fed, sleek black mare with the conformation of a thoroughbred. Alison stopped at a small clearing along the creek, deep-shadowed by willow thickets. "I came here to warn you, Jim Benton," she said, standing close. "Get away from here, before it's too late."

"You got me wrong, lady," Jim Benton said, flat-toned. "I have a job to do here."

"You can't do much with a bullet in your back. Get the hell away from this place." She was closer now, her red mouth all but touching his.

"Did Cass McCandless send you here to throw a scare into me?"

"If my husband found me here, like this," her voice tense, "he'd shoot you down and cut me to ribbons with a horse-whip."

Jim kept telling himself this while he fought against the trained seductiveness that made his heart pound and put a trembling weakness into his knees.

"There are women," her husky whisper was closer now, "that reach their pinnacle at thirty. I am that breed of female. Married to an old burnt-out shell of a man. Guarded day and night like an animal by his foreman, Lorne Mackin, as lecherous a bastard as ever drew breath." The animal heat of her long slender body reached him. "A woman gets hungry for a man," she whispered. Then she flung herself at him, her long fingernails clawing him.

The sudden savagery of her attack sent him reeling backwards, off balance. He saw the wild look in her eyes and felt her sobbing breath fan his face. Her teeth fastened in his lower lip, her body writhing against him.

The sharp crack of a 30-30 carbine sent flat echoes across the rolling prairie. As the waspish whine of a ricocheting bullet cut through the high willows, there was a second shot and a third. Then a man's hoarse scream knifed through the gunfire, followed by the pounding of thudding hoofs.

Jim Benton pulled away, saw the scream forming on her mouth, and his hand closed over the twisted lips.

He stood, half-crouched, the gun in his hand. Alison's horse was lunging and snorting at the sound of the gunfire and running horses. Jim made a quick grab for the bridle reins as the carelessly tied knot slipped off the brush. The lunging horse yanked him forward just as the deafening explosion of a .32 pistol in Alison's hand spat flame. Still hanging onto the bridle reins, he slapped the gun from her hand, using his own gun barrel in a swift chopping movement. She let out a sharp cry of pain and spat a nasty word at him.

He shoved his gun into its holster, and picking her up from the ground, he swung her into the saddle. "Whatever your game was," Jim Benton told her, "somebody gummed the cards." Holding the bridle reins, he rubbed his hand along his powder-burnt jaw, a grin twisting his mouth. "Tell Cass McCandless to come himself the next time," he said and handed her the reins, "instead of sending his wife."

"You fool," she said, low-toned. "Cass is in Texas. Lorne Mackin must have followed me here. To spy on me. I never meant to shoot you. The gun went off accidentally."

"That's how come you were about to holler rape," Jim Benton told her. He picked up the pocket pistol. "A hammerless gun don't go off by accident, lady. You had it made to shoot me and you'd fix up some lie that I tried to attack you." He emptied the gun and handed it back to her. Before she could think up an answer, he slapped the filly's rump with the flat of his hand. The startled animal almost jumped out from under her. When she regained her balance, she brought the riding crop down viciously across the horse's flanks and the mare broke into a run.

When she had disappeared, he saw a horsebacker ride out from behind the brush, a saddle gun in his hand. He was lowering the carbine as if he had had the rider in his gunsights and when he'd recognized Cass McCandless' wife, he had lowered the gun.

At the slight movement in the brush and the sound of a gun hammer being thumbed back, Jim Benton cocked his gun and fired at the sounds, quickly flattening himself to the ground before the other man fired. He heard the whine of the bullet over his head and fired again at the spit of gun flame. There was a guttural, harsh outcry and the crashing of brush. A horse snorted and a rider spurred out, lying low over the saddle horn and the neck of the running horse. Before Jim could take a snap shot, the rider was gone.

A moment later there was another roar of a gun. A high-pitched scream needled sharply through the gun echoes, followed by the splashing and the pounding of shod hoofs as the horsebacker spurred away. There was the pinging whine of barbwire being snapped as horse and rider crashed into the cross-fenced pasture. The harsh scream of the rider broke off abruptly, and as the horse stampeded towards the open gate, there was only the slapping of empty stirrups.

Jim Benton stood tracked in the willow thicket, his gun ready. From the direction of the dipping vat, he heard the sound of splashing and a choked outcry. He moved fast, crashing through the brush, with the cry for help from Speck dinning his ears.

When he reached the long concrete vat, the boy's head surfaced, arms flailing the murky black dip mixture. Jim reached in and grabbed the boy's shoulder, and it took all his strength to drag the drowning Speck up onto the catwalk along the vat. Gathering the limp and dripping boy in his arms, he headed for the lean-to shed with a long-legged stride. He kicked open the door and in the pitch dark, he laid him belly down on the army cot, letting his head hang over the edge.

He was moving his hands upward to assist the vomiting when he saw the outline of a man framed in the doorway. Jim slid one hand free and clawed for his gun.

"Hold your fire, Doc." The man's voice had the creaky sound of an old windmill. "I'm Chiz McDougal, Matt Wagner's pardner."

50

"Come in. Shut the door and light the lamp. I just dragged Speck out of the dipping vat." He put his gun back in the holster. "I'll have to work fast to get the poison out of his lungs and belly or he'll die." Jim Benton went back to work with big hands that moved with skilled swiftness, pulling the boy's belly from underneath and letting him vomit.

Old Chiz McDougal was a small, wiry, bowlegged man with a cross-grained leathery face and puckered blue eyes. He carried the lighted lamp in and put it down on the bench, and stood hipshot while Jim worked over Speck. When Jim asked him to fetch a pail of water and clean towel, he moved fast. He told Chiz to dipper water over the boy's head and wipe the muck off his face.

Both men worked without wasted motion, removing Speck's clothing and wiping the tobacco-brown slime off his body. When the vomiting ceased, Jim eased the boy over on his back so that his head lay on the clean towel Chiz had put under him.

Jim left and was back in a few seconds with a quart bottle of milky-looking liquid. The sick boy groaned and opened his bloodshot eyes. "You'll be all right, feller," Jim assured him. "Try to drink all this stuff. It tastes like whitewash, but hold it down as long as you can. When it comes up, it will bring all the muck with it and coat the lining of your stomach."

Speck tried to force a game grin. He swallowed the chalk-like antidote. In a few minutes the vomiting began again. When it was all over, Jim fed Speck a mixture of canned milk and water at intervals until the boy fell asleep. Jim and Chiz went outside, leaving the door open a few inches.

Old Chiz's blue eyes were frosty. He shifted his weight and jerked a thumb backwards. "One of the Spiderweb killers is hung up in the fence. Deader'n hell. Tried to ride his horse through and didn't make it. Has a wire wrapped around his throat like a necktie."

Jim Benton twisted a cigarette into shape and lit it before he spoke. "I swapped a couple of shots with him before he forked his horse. Whoever he was, he took a quick shot at Speck as he rode past and when the boy dodged he must have lost his balance and fell into the dipping vat."

"But it wasn't you who killed that big ox, Curly Mapes."

Jim Benton kept silent. Cowhands like Old Chiz McDougal told things in their own way.

"Curly Mapes' side-pardner, Skeeter Owens, was bushed up near the gate, and when he saw Mapes on the ground, he musta jumped him." Chiz looked off into the distant darkness. "Mapes' belly was ripped open and Skeeter wrapped a loose strand of barbwire around his neck and hung him to a fence post. Then he forked his horse and rode away."

"Why," Jim Benton said slowly, "murder one of his own outfit?"

"Those two have hated one another since I can remember," said Old Chiz. "Besides that, Curly was set afoot when his horse stampeded, and Skeeter figured he'd spill his guts if you worked him over. So he killed him."

"What was there to tell?" Jim Benton wanted to know.

"Plenty. Cass has some Spiderweb cattle coming up the trail from the Panhandle. He figures on bringing them into Montana, regardless of any quarantine regulations the Stockgrowers' Association might rule on," Chiz gritted. "That's why he wants a feller named Dr. Jim Benton, in charge of the Quarantine Station and maybe has a stock detective badge pinned to his undershirt, killed off."

Jim faced the cold scrutiny without

flinching, aware that there was something sticking in the old cowhand's craw from the start. "What's on your mind, Chiz?" he asked, grimly.

"Curly Mapes and Skeeter Owens weren't the only Spiderweb men here tonight. Lorne Mackin was cold-trailin' Cass' young wife."

"You hear about my run-in with the Spiderweb killers at the post office?" Jim Benton tried to keep the anger from his voice.

"Terry Wagner told me."

"Tonight Alison McCandless brought me the mail pouch they got away with and some of my personal letters," Jim said defiantly. Jim was thinking fast, wondering how much the tough old cowhand knew. He watched Chiz shift his weight, a habit of his.

"Maybe it's none of my business," Chiz said waspishly, "but your face is smeared with her red mouth paint and your face is clawed like you'd been tryin' to tame Frazier's wildcat."

"Go on," said Jim Benton through tight lips.

"Terry Wagner gave me one of her top horses to fetch here for you to use. That Redman gelding is in the barn." Chiz stood there, hipshot, with his hand on the wooden butt of his gun. "If ever you hurt Terry . . ."

The anger that had been building up inside Jim Benton was gone. "If that's the way you feel, have at it, Chiz," he said quietly, without a trace of malice. "But there's nothing between Cass McCandless' wife and me. I can't go into detail about the lip smear and the scratches. You'll have to take my word for it. Or call me a liar."

"You're not the breed of man to lie out of anything." He held out a gnarled hand.

Jim Benton gripped the proffered hand. "Some day," Jim said, smiling, "I'll be free to tell you about it. Right now I better get back to my patient. I wish you'd take the boy home with you, Chiz."

"I got it made to stay here with you, Doc," Chiz answered.

Old Chiz followed Jim inside. The boy's face was still white and drawn, but his eyes opened and he managed a grin. As Jim passed the shaving mirror, he saw his reflection and knew that Chiz had reason for everything he'd said. The first streaks of dawn were creeping into the skyline when Jim lifted the blanket-wrapped Speck in his arms and carried him to the big house.

"Blow out the lamp and fetch the mail

pouch, Chiz," Jim said, over his shoulder. "Shut the door when you come out."

When he had put Speck to bed and had covered him up, Speck said weakly, "I never made it to town, Dr. Jim. The letter's in my saddle pocket. When I saw Lorne Mackin and two horsebackers headed this way, I came back by the lower gate and put my horse in the barn." A small sigh escaped the boy. "I hid in the manger first and went out into the corrals. When the shootin' started and Curly Mapes rode past and saw me, he took a shot at me. My foot slipped and I fell into the dippin' vat from the catwalk. I was a goner when you fished me out."

Jim Benton went to the barn and was glad for the chance to be alone. Moments later he led a heavy-muscled roan gelding out into the daylight. Jim saddled and rode him around for a few minutes and knew he had never forked a better mannered and schooled cow horse.

The grin was still on his face when he came into the kitchen. "Redman's a real horse, Chiz."

"Terry raised him. Handled him easy as a colt and broke him to saddle without any abuse."

Jim sat down to the best breakfast he'd

56

ever remembered eating — ham and bacon, sourdough flapjacks, pan-fried spuds, and black coffee. When he had helped with dishes, Jim went into the front room and opened the mail pouch on a big table. His three letters, along with the others in the sack, had all been steamed open, read and resealed. And on each letter he detected the same musk perfume used by Alison McCandless.

There was one unstamped letter with his name on it. The square envelope had the Spiderweb brand embossed on it. He shoved it quickly into his pocket as Chiz entered the room. He slit open the letter from the Montana Stockgrowers' Association which was addressed to him. Enclosed was a copy of the notice the Association was sending to all cattlemen, whether members or not:

Upon receipt of this notice, you will round up all cattle on your range and have them dipped for the eradication of cattle ticks. You have your choice of constructing your own dipping vats and mixing your own dip under the supervision of an experienced man approved by the U.S. Department of Agriculture, and sent out at government expense.

If any cattleman does not wish to go to the expense of constructing his own vats according to the enclosed blueprint of the specified design, he can dip his cattle at the most convenient U.S. Department of Agriculture Experimental Station. This can be done by notifying the man in charge, giving him a rough estimate of the number of cattle to be dipped and the date of arrival.

"All cattle in the advanced stages of tick fever shall be promptly destroyed and buried in six-foot pits. This will be done on your own range and the records kept. Your herds will be inspected beforehand by a livestock inspector who will cut any cattle in the advanced stages of tick fever. Culling these cattle in advance can save time and money.

Any cattleman or any of his employees will be subject to arrest if he interferes in any way with the program to eradicate the cattle tick. Such interference will be subject to a fine or imprisonment or both, and all cattle in your brand shall be impounded.

Jim Benton read the notice, then handed it to Chiz. "This thing has teeth in it, Chiz."

Jim Benton had given a lecture at the

Stockgrowers' Association meeting on methods of eradicating the Texas Tick, by dipping and leaving the range idle, free of livestock for perhaps a year. A motion had been passed to quarantine the State of Montana against the entrance of all cattle from Texas and all other states known to be infested with ticks.

Cass McCandless had been at that meeting and strongly opposed the State quarantine. He was rabid in the speeches he'd made and the irate Spiderweb owner had to be removed from the meeting.

Both the notice and the contents of the letters were no news to Jim Benton. He'd had it by word of mouth a week ago. But seeing it in black and white made it official.

"You got a bull by the bushy tail, Doc?" Old Chiz McDougal's creaky voice sounded behind him.

It put a grin on Jim's face. He hitched up his cartridge belt. His eyes were bleak when he said, "McCandless and his Spiderweb outfit is a big hunk of tough, raw meat to chaw on, Chiz."

"Sounds easy when some white-collared dude in Washington writes it down on paper," Old Chiz said as he slapped the notice against a horny palm and tossed it on the table. "But Cass McCandless is a hard man to shave. He ain't goin' to the trouble and expense of buildin' a dippin' vat, and he won't round up the cattle and drive them in here for dippin'. What you goin' to do about it, Doc?"

"There's a lot of government red tape to be cut, Chiz. When that's done, I'll figure something out." Jim Benton picked up the Association notice. "Judging from this," he said, "McCandless has been notified by mail. I'm checking the bet to the Spiderweb. In the meantime, I'll get rid of the ticky cattle right here and get the dipping outfit in shape and fresh supplies in."

"There's a hellslue of Texas cattle on the way, Doc. The big ranges down in Texas are overstocked and Cass McCandless has been buying up everything he can at his own price and trailin' them here."

"Before they reach Montana, the State Quarantine law will be passed. That'll stop him."

"McCandless washed his hands and polished his boots in spilled blood during the Fence Cutters' War," said Old Chiz. "He built up his big herds and a tough rep in No Man's Land and the Indian Territory. Cass McCandless is much man wherever you want to put him."

"Even here in Montana?"

"Even here in Montana. So far, he's managed to keep his hands clean. He hires killers like Lorne Mackin to do his dirty work." Old Chiz spat disgustedly. "When a tough gunslinger like Curly Mapes gets killed, he brings another one up from Tascosa."

"Cass McCandless is bucking Uncle Sam on this deal, Chiz."

"McCandless bucked the Texas Rangers down in the Panhandle," Chiz said grimly. "He don't know how it feels to be scared."

Jim Benton's lopsided grin raised a skeptical eyebrow. "I got a look at him at the Association meeting. A big, red-faced, loud-mouthed bulldozer who stunk up the place with his whisky breath and was put out when he got irate."

Chiz nodded, then measured his words. "Cass McCandless is a man who tells somebody he's going to kill him. Then when the sign is right, keeps his word."

"You wouldn't be throwing a big scare into a man, Chiz?"

"Nope. You don't scare worth a damn, Doc. I'm only tellin' you what you're up against. You'll need help. Plenty of it and a lot of luck. You're not damn fool enough to tackle the Spiderweb alone, even with

61

the backin' of Uncle Sam."

"I'm a damn fool, all right," Jim Benton's grin spread. "I can prove that. But not that big a damn fool, Chiz." He picked up his hat off the floor and went outside, closing the door behind him.

He walked over to the cowshed lab. Lighting the lamp, he took the square envelope from his pocket. He slit it open and removed a single sheet of paper that smelled of musk perfume. Attached to the paper was a check on a Butte bank made out to James Benton for $25,000. It was signed by Alison McCandless. Two printed words filled the paper: QUIT MONTANA!

III

Jim Benton sent Old Chiz McDougal to Sundown with the delayed letter to Dr. Rosene Spencer at Hamilton, with the same instructions he had given Speck — to deliver it in person to the stage driver, Hank Sanford. He told Chiz to notify the coroner about the dead man at the Quarantine Station and to tell him to fetch his hearse and enough solid citizens of Sundown to make up a coroner's jury. He handed Chiz a new padlock and key. "Lock the gate when you go out. Keep the key. I have a duplicate."

It was a little past noon when Speck sighted the cloud of dust. "Yonder they come, Doc," he called.

"Better get inside, feller," Jim said. "If I need you, I'll let you know."

Jim Benton shoved the Winchester carbine into the saddle scabbard and rode slowly toward the padlocked gate. He leaned from the saddle and unlocked the padlock and swung the gate open. He sat his horse to one side of the gate.

Two men rode in the lead of the old

black hearse. Felix Carruthers in his swallowtail coat sat beside the driver from the livery barn. Four men rode in pairs behind, with Old Chiz bringing up the rear. When he sighted Jim Benton, he lifted his Winchester from across the front of his saddle in a grim salute.

Jim's hand was on his gun as he halted the procession at the gate. Carruthers' face had a gray look and he kept cracking the knuckles of both hands.

"Any man has a gun on him," Jim Benton said quietly, "drop it at the gate."

"They all pack guns, Doc," Chiz called out. "I made 'em put 'em in the dead wagon. Ain't a Spiderweb man in the outfit, except that bald-headed buzzard in the claw-hammer coat."

"Where's the corpse?" Felix snapped with annoyance.

"Hung up on a fence at the corrals," Old Chiz answered, "where his pardner, Skeeter Owens, left the gutted ox."

"Get goin'." Felix jabbed a sharp elbow into the driver's ribs.

"Lorne Mackin's in town, fixin' to get drunker'n seven hundred dollars," Chiz told Jim. "Skeeter's followin' him like a shrunk-up shadow. The clerk at the hotel says Cass McCandless' wife has been locked in the suite Cass rents by the year. Been there since late last night. Has her meals sent up and a sawed-off, double-barreled scatter gun and a box of shells in her room."

"Any other news?" Jim prompted.

"They say Cass' wife, without him knowing anything about it, hired herself a smart lawyer and got legal claim to half the Spiderweb outfit. From that day on Cass has dealt her unshirted hell. He pays his ramrod, Lorne Mackin, to watch her. If he catches her in a compromisin' position with another man, he can kick her tail to hell out and get back her half of the Spiderweb outfit. That's what damn nigh happened last night. Mackin brought along two eye-witnesses."

"Let's have the rest of it, Chiz."

"Skeeter Owens claims that him and Curly Mapes caught you and her together last night. When Mapes showed up, you shot him. He managed to crawl to his horse and make a run for it, but his horse fouled up in the fence and threw him. When he landed in the barbwire, you finished the job with a knife."

"And Felix Carruthers, who takes his orders from the Spiderweb, will reach a quick verdict, and I'll be accused of the

65

murder of Curly Mapes."

"That's about the size of it, Doc."

Jim Benton spurred his horse and headed for the scene of the inquest.

Felix Carruthers was saying, "We'll bury the corpse here. We'll discuss the findings of the jury in the courtroom in Sundown." His watery eyes flicked a glance at Jim Benton.

"Not so fast, Mister Coroner," Jim Benton said. "This is government property. Unless you have a permit for burial, signed by me or some other duly authorized government officer, you will place the dead man in the hearse and take him to town. Is that plain?" Jim eyed the coroner down.

From the tail pocket of his coat, Felix Carruthers took a pair of white cotton gloves. He reached inside the hearse to drag out a pine box covered with black cheesecloth. "Lend a hand with the corpse, jurymen," he said pompously.

"Not me," a short, paunchy juryman said. "Not us," he elaborated. "We draw down five bucks for jury duty, not to handle the dead. You get paid twenty-five bucks, Felix. Ten more for the use of your hearse and five for a man to drive. Earn your money, Felix." The speaker looked up at Chiz, then at Jim Benton. "All right if we get our six-shooters from the coffin, Chiz?"

"It's up to the boss." Chiz jerked a thumb toward Jim.

"That depends," Jim said, "on what the jury's verdict is on how the corpse met his death."

"As official coroner," Felix Carruthers cut in, "the findings of this jury will be discussed in my courtroom in Sundown."

A grim smile flattened Jim Benton's lips into a white line.

"Load your dead wagon, Carruthers," Jim Benton said gruffly, "and get out. Take your jurymen with you." Jim turned toward Chiz. "If you think you can handle them, Chiz," he said in a low tone, "I'll get on back to the house."

"Hell, yes, Doc."

Speck opened the door when Jim Benton rode up. He had a carbine in the crook of his arm. "If them fellers had a-started a ruckus, Doc, I was goin' to get in my six-bits' worth."

"Thanks, Speck." They watched the black hearse until it went through the gate. There was no sign of the half-dozen jurymen or of Old Chiz. Jim Benton was puzzled until he saw all of them ride up to the house. He stepped outside.

"I talked to these fellers," Chiz gestured toward the six men sitting their horses uneasily, "into stayin'. They all got cattle in their own irons, their brands registered. Lorne Mackin's been feedin' 'em a pack of damn lies. I told 'em you'd be glad to explain the cattle dippin' deal to 'em, Doc."

"Sure thing, Chiz. Be glad to." He looked at the men on horseback. "It's part of my job, men."

The short, heavy-paunched jury foreman edged his horse over to Jim Benton who was standing beside Speck. He swung down from the saddle. "It didn't take much argument from Old Chiz to get us to stay. We all got families. None of us can afford to buck the Spiderweb outfit," he explained. "I'm Bill Irvin. Used to ramrod what we called the Nester Pool till the Spiderweb took over the range."

Jim Benton shoved out a hand as the man hesitated. "Glad to know you, Bill." He smiled grimly. "I know what you're up against."

The other five men swung down and shook hands, introducing themselves.

Bill Irvin studied Jim Benton for a long moment, then turned to a long-legged cowpuncher about thirty, and said, "Maybe you better tell him yourself, Slim."

Jim Benton saw the shadow of worry in the slim man's eyes.

"I got no right to ask you, Doc," Slim began, rubbing his stubbled jaw roughly. "I know you're a vet, not the kind of doctor my wife needs. But it's her first baby. I'm scared. Scared as hell, Doc," he blurted.

The hard core inside Jim Benton broke and spilled warmth through his veins. He'd helped his father bring a few babies into the world, but it had been a long time ago.

"Where is your wife, Slim?" he asked.

"At the ranch, across Grasshopper. About six miles from here as the crow flies. Ten by wagon road."

"We'll take the short cut." Jim turned to Chiz. "You're in charge till I get back. You and Speck. Show these men what the dipping is all about." He turned and went into the house.

He opened his suitcase and took out his father's black doctor's bag. He scanned the contents hurriedly, his face flushed from inner excitement.

"Let's get going, Slim," Jim Benton said, as he stepped outside. He tied the bag on his saddle and mounted Redman.

"We'll have to cut a couple government fences, Doc," Slim said, as they rode away.

"We'll swing by the barn. I saw some wire cutters there."

Chiz and Speck and the five nester cowmen watched them when they came to the first fence. Slim swung down with the wire cutters, snapped the five taut wires, then they rode off at a long trot.

"By gawdamighty," Bill Irvin said fervently, "yonder goes a man."

As Jim Benton and Slim rode up to the cabin, a gray-haired woman stood in the doorway.

"That's Bill Irvin's missus," said Slim.

"Sarah's having labor pains, Slim," the woman said.

"This is Doctor Benton, Miz Irvin."

"Thank God, Doctor."

The two men dismounted and Jim Benton carried his black bag to the cabin. Mrs. Irvin stood aside to let the two men enter.

A delicate girl, with a mass of brown hair spread on the white pillow, lay swollen with child under the clean sheet and light-weight blanket. Her eyes were pain-glazed, her lips pale and trembling as she forced a smile.

"It's all right, honey." Slim's voice was unsteady as he kissed her. "I brought a doctor . . . Doc Benton."

It was nearly an hour later that Slim's wife was suckling a baby boy at her swollen breasts.

Jim's hands were a little unsteady as he put the sterilized instruments back into the bag. With the last rays of the setting sun flooding the room from the window, Jim had felt his father's presence beside him. It was a strange feeling that crept into him.

"You'll want some coffee, Doctor, and warm food before you start back," he vaguely heard the woman say. When she started moving about, he turned away from the window and picked up his bag. "I'll eat when I get back to the Quarantine Station. Tell Slim I'll be back sometime tomorrow."

Jim Benton left the house quietly, saddled the roan, and rode away as the evening star came into being in the dark purple sky. He let his horse follow the wagon road, taking the longer route back. He wanted those hours to himself, to let the darkness creep in and to let the stars come down within reach.

Jim Benton was riding through country that had history and legend. Here on Grasshopper Creek, where he stopped to

71

let Redman drink at the gravel crossing, gold had been discovered in 1862. The backwash of prospectors from the California gold fields followed the rainbow trail of the gold rush into the boom town of Bannack. The town had mushroomed overnight into a roaring placer camp and later became the capital of Montana Territory.

Road agents had preyed on the miners with the pick and shovel and gold pans. Henry Plummer had organized his notorious Plummer gang, with George Ives the right hand bower of the archvillain. The Vigilantes came into existence here. Later they hanged Plummer from his own buildings at Bannack, and soon thereafter the rest of the gang was caught and dealt the same fate as Plummer.

It was at Bannack that Dr. Hugh Benton, a young man fresh from medical school, had hung up his shingle. When the gold rush moved on, Dr. Benton migrated with the gold seekers, finally settling down at Last Chance Gulch, later the town of Helena. There he built himself a house, took a wife, and sank his tap roots. Jim Benton was born at Helena.

Jim Benton had grown up in the legend of the country. Riding alone, but never alone in the silence of the vast country, he watched the moon push up over the broken skyline. Never was he more keenly aware of the heritage that was his birthright than he was now.

The night was warm and scented with sage greasewood. Redman traveled at a running walk on the road that crossed a prairie-dog town that stretched for a mile or more on Alkali flat. The crossing brought back nostalgic memories. Hank Sanford had pointed out the old tumbled-down cabin where Dr. Benton had first practiced.

Perhaps because Jim's inner thoughts had dwelt on bygone Vigilante days, the high crossbeam of the pole gate at the big gate took on a gallows-like appearance, even to the shadowy form of a dangling body on the end of a rope. Jim smiled faintly, telling himself it was some trick of the night shadows playing on his imagination.

It was only when Redman lifted his head, ears pricked forward and nostrils flared, and slowed to a stiff-legged gait, that reality came back to Jim. In that split second of danger, reflex action put a gun in his hand. The big roan halted, spooked, its tail grabbed. The rider sat tensely, knees gripping, the reins in his left hand and his gun in his right.

One look was enough to identify the hanged man. There was no mistaking the motionless figure of Felix Carruthers in the long black, claw-hammer coat.

Jim circled the buildings and corrals warily, keeping to the shadows of the tall willows along the creek. No light showed at the main house and there was no sign of life.

"Stand your hand!" The voice cracked like a pistol shot. "Ride out with your hands up!" Old Chiz's voice scraped like a saw rifle.

"Hold it, Chiz!" Jim Benton rode into the moonlight.

Chiz limped out from behind one of the corrals, a Winchester cradled in the crook of his arm.

"What's been going on around here?" Jim's voice was edged.

"A wake," Chiz said. His lined face broke into a grin. "A gawddamned wake for Felix Carruthers. Felix rode his hearse to his own funeral." Chiz nodded in the direction of the barn. "It's over by the barn where Lorne Mackin's cowhands dragged it with ketch-ropes. Damnedest performance a man ever watched."

"Where's Speck?"

"Hid out in the brush."

"Where's Bill Irvin and the other nesters?"

"Bill's bushed up somewhere. The others pulled out for home."

Bill Irvin, followed by Speck, came out of the brush. Both carried carbines. Little by little, Jim Benton got the story of the hanging of Felix Carruthers.

Five of the jurymen had gone back home late that afternoon. Bill Irvin said he'd stay until Jim returned. They had just finished supper shortly after dark when they heard a lot of hollering outside the padlocked gate. It looked like a Spiderweb invasion, so they put out the light and waited behind locked doors. Chiz had sent Speck upstairs where he'd be safer. The boy had found a pair of army field glasses up there and Chiz went up to view the whole thing through the powerful binoculars that brought the scene close.

Somebody shot off the padlock and swung the gate wide open. Felix was sitting, ramrod stiff, on the seat of the hearse. There was a rope tied to the crossbeam of the gate and Skeeter Owens was on top of the hearse fixing the hangman's knot. Several riders had their ketch-ropes tied to the wagon tongue and dallied around their saddle horns. A whisky bottle passed from hand to hand.

From the upstairs window Chiz and Speck heard Lorne Mackin's voice. "You had a bench warrant for Jim Benton, Carruthers, and six men to back you up when you served it. But you never served it. You came back to town without the six men. We let you bury Curly Mapes and then we unhooked the livery team and the boys hauled your wagon here. The boys will drag it to the door of that big white house and you can serve that bench warrant on Benton, and we'll bring him back to the gate. You'll hold court here and Benton will be tried and convicted for the murder of Curly Mapes. We'll hang him to his own damn government gate, and you'll still be Mayor and Judge and Postmaster at Sundown. But this is your last chance, you bald-headed old buzzard. Take it or leave it."

Chiz said Felix Carruthers managed to stand up and in a loud voice, he shouted, "Hear ye! Thieves and vandals and murderers! I have never condoned murder! I shall take no part in the murder of James Benton. If this be my last act on earth, then so be it!" Felix tore the bench warrant into shreds and threw the handful of paper into Skeeter's face.

Skeeter dropped the noose over the bald head and jerked the rope tight around the skinny throat. Taking the long black whip from the socket on the dashboard, he lashed out at the rumps of the saddled horses. The sudden jump all but threw the riders. As the hearse moved swiftly out from under Carruthers, Skeeter jumped to the ground. The raiders dragged the hearse up to the barn and turned their dallies loose and loped off, leaving their ketch-ropes tied to the wagon tongue.

Jim Benton nodded in thoughtful silence. He told Bill Irvin he'd better head for Slim Smith's place, in case any of the Spiderweb cowhands chose to drop in there.

When he had ridden away, Jim had Speck hook the mule team to the ambulance. He took Chiz with him to cut down and bury the dead man.

IV

That day Jim Benton, with the assistance of Chiz and Speck, rounded up the quarantined cattle. Each critter had a number painted on its hide designating how many times it had been dipped. In a vest pocket tally book Jim Benton had copied the number of dipped cattle from the ledger in the lab, jotting down the dates.

"In spite of Lorne Mackin and his tough hands and their damned fool efforts to block the experiments, the results are there, Chiz. Even the ones that still need one or more dippings are in good shape."

The two men sat their horses at the edge of the herd and Chiz agreed with what Jim said.

Jim Benton told Speck to day herd the cattle while he and Chiz did the dipping. "Keep an eye open for horse-backers, Speck," he added, "while we dip the ticky cattle we've penned."

Both men watched the boy as he rode away to scatter the cattle out and let them graze. For all the hot soapy water, the boy's body was tinged a light tobacco brown. His straw-colored hair was stained a darker brown. Other than that he had come out without a trace of illness from the arsenic dip.

"They don't come any better than that speckled-faced kid, Doc," Old Chiz said. "His old man was a top hand. Had a wild streak, though. He'd a wound up travelin' the outlaw trail only he met a girl and married her. Whitey Carver killed three Spiderweb gunslingers before they got him." Old Chiz spat in the dust. "Speck's carryin' his old man's gun. One of these days he's liable to use it. That's how come I gotta ride close herd on him."

It took until late afternoon for the two men to run the cattle through the dipping vat. While the dip was drying, Chiz waved Speck in with his hat and they ate a cold dinner.

At sunset they hazed the little bunch of dipped cattle into the bigger herd and the three of them herded the cattle for the big gate. Jim and Chiz tallied them through the gate while Spec kept the drags moving. When all the cattle had been turned loose to scatter on Spiderweb range, they sighted a lone horsebacker approaching in the distance. As the rider came closer, both Jim

79

and Chiz recognized Cass McCandless' wife.

"Me'n' the boy will ride back to the house, Doc." Chiz motioned Speck with his head and they rode away.

Jim Benton rolled a cigarette as he watched Alison McCandless approach. He lit it and thumbed back his hat from his rust-colored hair. Dust and sweat dirtied his face and his clothes were stained brown with cattle dip.

Alison had changed from her riding habit into a silk blouse and a divided skirt of brown suede. A gray Stetson covered her blonde hair. Dust powdered her face. Her mouth was a crimson slash, her long eyes, glass-green. In a saddle boot she packed a 30-30 carbine. The opened neck of her blouse showed part of a leather shoulder holster and the bulge of a gun showed under her blouse. She reined her horse alongside his, stirrups touching. There was no warmth in her eyes as she looked at him.

Jim Benton was tight as a coiled spring. He had pulled off his hat and forced a grin.

For a long time they sat their saddles like that. He was checking the bet to her. In spite of the dust and the tiny beads of perspiration under her eyes and on her upper lip, she was the most exotic and beautiful woman he had ever laid eyes on. He wondered if the pounding vein in his temple showed.

Her red lips peeled back to show clenched teeth. The laugh that came from behind the teeth was short. It reminded Jim of the square envelope in his hip pocket and he reached for it. It was crumpled and damp, as he removed the check and handed it to her.

She took it in one of her gauntleted hands. He watched her take a cigarette from a silver case and put it between her lips. Instead of leaning forward to light the cigarette from the match he held cupped in his hand, she twisted the check and held one end in the match flame, then lit her cigarette with it. Tilting her head, she pulled the tobacco smoke deep and when the check had burned to ashes, she laughed again in the same brittle way.

"Twenty-five thousand dollars." Her voice was low and husky. "That's the price Cass McCandless paid for me." Her smile twisted. "I tried to buy you with it." Her eyes narrowed slightly, as she asked, "What's marked on your price tag, Benton?"

He tried to read what was in her eyes, but he gave up after a long moment. "I don't get it, lady. If Cass McCandless wants to buy me, why don't he make the offer himself? That threat in your note don't scare me worth a damn."

"That note said to quit Montana. I was buying you with my own money. At the time I wrote it, I fully intended going with you. Any place on the face of the earth as long as we rode together off the Spiderweb range." Her eyes darkened in the shadow of the wide hat brim. "Do I make myself plain, Benton?"

"There's more to it," Jim said bluntly. "Lay your cards face up."

Alison pulled smoke into her lungs and let it drift out with the words. "Apart from the fact that I wanted you, if anything should happen to my husband, his share of the Spiderweb would go to his widow. Are you following me, Benton?"

"I'm way ahead of you, lady," Jim Benton said flatly. "You want me to kill your husband. Marry his widow, to get a dead man's share of his ranch."

"You put it bluntly. But you hit the bull's-eye. If I had a nickel cigar, I'd give it to you."

Jim laid both hands on his saddle horn.

"You got the wrong man. But I can name a man who would smoke that nickel cigar down and eat the butt. Why don't you take it up with Lorne Mackin?"

"It was Mackin's idea to start with." Her red mouth twisted. "He propositioned me the first time Cass left him to ride herd on me when he went to Texas."

"You should have taken Mackin up," Jim retorted with brutal frankness.

"I asked for that one, Benton," Alison said. Spacing her words carefully, she added, "Ask Mackin some time to show you the bullet scar that tore off part of a rib. That was my answer to him."

"I spoke out of turn. I'm sorry."

"Skip it, Benton." She forced a smile. "I'm a gal who takes a lot of knowing and you're not the breed of man to ever understand about women." When she looked up at him, the glint was back in her eyes. They were cold and calculating.

"When Lorne Mackin and Skeeter finished painting the town red last night, they pounded on my hotel room door with their six-shooters and told me to open up. They'd had orders from Cass to frame me in a compromising position. I had the sawed-off shotgun that the Wells Fargo guard used to pack on the stage. I cocked both hammers, pointed the double barrels at the door and pulled the triggers. I could hear Skeeter yelping like a wounded coyote as I went out through the window and down a post." She was silent for a while as she drew smoke into her lungs. Pinching the cigarette out, she flipped it to the ground.

"Hank Sanford had my black mare tied behind the barn," she continued. "He was waiting when I got there. He told me to hide out at the old stage station near Bannack and he'd pick me up around midnight tonight. I'll turn the mare loose and ride the stage to the railroad and catch the first train out."

She looked steadily at Jim. "I'm quitting the Spiderweb while the going's good, Benton. I'm signing over my half interest in the Spiderweb outfit to a man named Jim Benton. My attorney will draw up the necessary papers and he'll see to it that nothing can take it away from you."

Alison crowded her horse close and held out her hand. "Here's where our trails fork." The grip of her fingers was hard as a man's handclasp. "Good-bye and good luck, Doctor James Benton."

Before Jim could find the words he wanted, she slid her hand from his, whirled the mare around and was gone in a cloud of dust.

"Good-bye and good luck," he muttered, staring after her until horse and rider disappeared from sight in the early twilight.

He'd need luck, a hell of a lot of it. Whenever Cass McCandless got the news that his wife had signed her half interest in the Spiderweb to him, Jim Benton, he'd be needing a hell of a lot more than just luck. When Alison put her name to that paper, she would be signing Jim Benton's death warrant.

Alison hadn't made any brazen pass at him. He couldn't figure her out. He recalled her remark that she didn't think he was the breed of man who would ever understand about women. She was one hundred per cent right. No argument about that.

Her move had not been an impulsive one. She had made him a cold-blooded proposition to kill her husband. Murder was a big price to pay for a beautiful body and a share in a million dollar cattle spread. Failing in her first attempt, Alison had played her ace in the hole. Jim Benton would have to kill Cass McCandless before Cass put a bounty on his hide and ordered him killed by his gunslingers. She packed a two-edged dagger. She'd left it stuck in Jim Benton's gizzard and had ridden away.

That smart lawyer she had mentioned would see to it that win, lose or draw, Alison would get her widow's share, if not the entire holdings of the Spiderweb outfit in Texas and Montana. There was a hell of a lot of truth in that timeworn statement about a woman scorned.

Jim Benton swung the pole gate shut and rode back. He wasn't relishing looking Old Chiz in the eye when he made up some plausible lie for Alison McCandless' visit.

The three men and the boy took one-hour turns standing guard that morning while the others of the Nester Pool slept.

Bone-tired as he was, Jim Benton slept fitfully, and those brief hours were troubled by jumbled dreams. There was too much on his mind. His job was to get the Quarantine Station in readiness, check the fences and concrete vat, the cleated runways and the dripping pens and the supplies. He had to get word to the Spiderweb and every little cowman in his district, giving them approximate dates their cattle would be dipped. They had to be notified to round up their cattle and hold them in readiness, or suffer the penalties that would be imposed. And right now he was shorthanded for help.

Long before dawn he was up and checking the warehouse supplies. As near as he could estimate in advance there were enough dipping solution materials to last throughout the season: white arsenic, caustic soda, lye, sodium carbonate, and pine tar.

Chiz and Speck showed up just as he'd finished checking the supplies. "There's enough ingredients here to make the S.B. dip," Jim told them.

That got a chuckle out of Chiz. "I can name you some Spiderweb S.B.'s that need dippin'," he said.

Jim grinned. "S.B. means self-boiled, Chiz," he enlightened the old cowhand. "I'll have to attend to the boiling myself. The dip solution will have to be mixed in the open and handled carefully." He scowled at the unlocked warehouse door. "This place should be padlocked."

"I looked around, Doc. Didn't find a padlock on the place."

"Remind me to get locks the next time I go to town," Jim said, and headed for the dipping vat.

He looked down at the stale brown mixture that had been there too long. The vat had no drain pipe outlet and it looked as if he and Chiz and Bill Irvin, who was relieving Chiz guarding the gate, would have to man some bailing buckets at the end of ropes.

Jim sent Speck out to the gate to relieve Irvin while he and Chiz went on the prowl for buckets. They were hunting in the wagon shed when they found an old iron pump and a couple lengths of pipe. It was what they needed. The three men set the pump in operation and took turns at the pump handle. In an hour the vat was pumped out.

"We'll let the sun dry it out," Jim said, "while we knock off for dinner."

Jim had ruined an old pair of Levi's and a fairly good shirt messing around with a scrub brush on a long handle. His face and hair were brown-spattered. He stripped and washed himself off in the creek. He was in water to his armpits when he heard a horsebacker coming through the high willows. His belt and gun were on the bank with the clean clothes he'd brought from the house. Before he had time to reach for the gun, the gay sound of a girl's laugh sent him into deeper water. His first thought that it was Alison McCandless was dispelled a few minutes later.

"That darned Old Chiz, sending me down here to find you." It was Terry Wagner's voice. "I'll get even with that old rannihan if it takes a month of Sundays."

"What fetches you to the Quarantine Station, Terry?" There was a trace of annoyance in the question.

"I brought you a few head of horses. Figured you might need a change," she said, then added, "I'll turn my back while you get dressed."

When Terry had ridden her horse behind the willows, Jim dressed and buckled on his gun. "You can come out now, Terry," he called out.

Jim caught his breath as he watched her walk toward him. She was slim as a boy, her cheeks flushed, eyes sparkling. Her hat was shoved back on her mop of curly black hair and her smile was worth a long day's ride.

She came within arms' reach before she halted. "You look like you aren't glad to see me, scowling like a cinnamon bear."

"You're the most beautiful sight a man ever looked at, Terry," Jim said in a husky voice. He reached out and pulled her into his arms. Her lips were warm and soft, trembling a little as he kissed her.

"I love you, Jim," she whispered softly.

After a while she pulled away. "What really fetched me here," she explained to cover her embarrassment at what she had said, "was to ask you if you'd come to the ranch and look at Big Red. He's down sick."

"What are we waiting for?" He kissed her hand and let her go. "Get your horse. Tell me the symptoms so I'll know what to put in the saddle bags."

Terry led her horse and told Jim about the sick stud horse as they walked to the house.

Speck came out of the barn, a grin on his speckled face. "Howdy, Sis," he said. "I hid in the barn when I saw you coming. I figured you'd come to drag me home."

"Wrong, Speck. Big Red's sick. I came for Jim to see if he can get him back on his feet."

"Doc'll do it if any man can," Speck bragged. Then he said to Jim, "Don't worry, Doc. Me'n' Chiz and Bill Irvin will take care of things till you get back."

"Keep the lab padlocked, feller," Jim told Speck. "And you better nail that warehouse door shut, Chiz."

Jim saddled Redman, and as they rode away, Speck called after them, "Next time, Sis, bring the buckboard."

They were nearing the horse pasture of

the Wagner ranch when the sharp crack of a 30-30 Winchester blasted the quiet. A cowbell clanged. Jim Benton's carbine was out of its saddle scabbard before the echoes of the gun shot died away.

"That's Dad at his target practice," Terry informed him. Then she cupped her hands to her mouth and lifted her voice. "It's Terry, Dad. I've fetched the vet."

While Terry leaned from her saddle to fit her key into the padlock on the gate, Jim Benton examined the cowbell that hung down from a rope to about a horsebacker's chest. The bell was dented on both flat sides where countless steel-jacketed bullets had hit it. When they had ridden through and closed and locked the gate, Jim gauged the distance from the gate to the log cabin. He judged it to be a hundred-yard range.

"Your father must be a good shot, Terry. Is he totally blind?"

"Sometimes. Other times, it's a gray world with black shadows. He uses whisky to ease the pain a little."

"I have some pills I can leave to deaden the pain," Jim said.

"Matt's afraid of pain-killing pills. Scared he'll get the drug habit."

"I'll talk it over with him."

As they neared the barn, a half dozen big

hounds came charging out from the wide-open doors. The two older dogs, one a bitch, were as big as a small shetland pony. They were broad between the eyes, heavy jawed, with battle scars and ragged ears. The bitch was short-haired, slate gray, the mastiff strain predominating. The male was wire-haired, shaggy, with the head and long jaws of an Irish wolfhound. Neither of them barked or made any whimpering sound of welcome. They were both stiff-legged, hackles raised, padding warily, as if ready to spring at a split-second warning.

"Don't reach for a gun, Jim," Terry warned.

The four pups showed the cross breed. They barked a couple of times as they came out of the barn, white fangs showing as they surrounded the two riders, holding them in a savage circle until the two older dogs came up.

There was an uneasy moment when Jim Benton half-expected the two older dogs to leap for his throat and drag him from the saddle. The dogs were killers.

"Don't step down, Jim. Keep both hands on your saddle horn like I have mine. If you pulled a gun, Duke and Duchess would tear you to pieces."

"Don't worry about my stepping down,"

Jim assured her. "How about you?"

"Matt trains the dogs. Chiz or Speck and I are the clay pigeons on horseback. Until the pups finish their training, I'm a stranger on horseback." Her faint smile left the shadow of worry in her eyes. "Something's wrong," she whispered.

A tall, raw-boned man, with a carefully trimmed gray beard and mustache and bushy hair came from the darkness of the barn. An old cartridge belt slanted across his lean flanks. A six-shooter was in a tied-down holster on his thigh. He carried a long-barreled rifle in the crook of his arm. Cold, steely eyes peered from under shaggy brows. His face was the color and texture of saddle leather.

"It's me, Dad," Terry said. "I've brought Doctor Benton from the Quarantine Station with me. He's going to take a look at Big Red."

"All right, Duke, Duchess," Matt Wagner spoke to the two big dogs, "take your pups and go to the dugout."

The dogs headed for the cellar dug in the side hill between the barn and the house. A slanting trap-door stood open, propped against a short post. The big dogs disappeared, followed by the four pups.

Jim and Terry dismounted. "Where's

that nester who was to stay here until I got back?" Terry asked, the worry back in her eyes.

"Gone," Matt said quietly. "He's long gone."

"What happened to him?"

"Duke and Duchess didn't like him. Something about the long-geared nester smelled bad and I felt the same way about him. I think he had it made to kill me."

The blind man hesitated a minute, then added, "I was in the box stall with Big Red when this nester said he'd go up into the loft and fork down some hay. I knew once he got up there he'd have the bulge, so I gave the dogs the signal to hold him. I warned him not to reach for his gun, but he did anyhow. That was a bad mistake. By the time I got the dogs off, he was in bad shape."

"He's dead." Terry made it a flat statement.

"Dead enough to bury." The cowman's voice was cold when he added, "He must have mixed some poison with the barley and oat mash, but the stud didn't eat much of it before he laid down sick."

Jim Benton went into the stall and examined the grain box in the manger. He could see the white arsenic powder that had been mixed with the mash. He felt sure it had come from the Quarantine Station. He twisted the box loose and carried it outside and buried it deep in the manure pile.

Terry looked at him with stricken eyes when he came back into the barn. She had lit the lantern and had hung it on a peg inside the stall.

"I'd be lying if I told you Big Red is going to live, Terry," Jim said. "But it's lucky he didn't eat much of the mash and there's a chance of saving him. We'll know in four or five hours. It's going to be an all-night job, so try to tough it out."

Terry nodded, still too choked up to trust her voice. There were tears in her eyes.

Jim asked her to get a bucket of warm water and about a pound of salt. He was going to give the stud a salt drench through the nostrils. Then he would get the stuff up through a stomach pump.

From then on it was a battle against death. Terry watched Jim slowly insert a long rubber tube into the horse's mouth and down into the stomach. When she saw him put one end of the tube into his own mouth and begin to suck, she caught her breath. But it was the only way. A minute later he spat out some slimy stuff and let the rest empty into a bucket. Terry brought him a dipperful of fresh drinking water which he gargled and spat until his mouth felt clean.

The stud was bloated. His breathing was rapid and froth slobbered from his open mouth. Jim gave the horse a hypodermic. Shortly afterwards he thumbed an eyelid back and bent close to examine the horse's eye. The big stud's forelegs were quivering. Jim watched the hind legs for a long moment and began kneading the muscles with professional skill. Then he administered warm water and mineral oil to rid the horse of the bloat.

There was a troubled look in the girl's eyes. "If I'd known it would turn out this way," she said, "I'd have fetched Chiz."

Jim reached for her hand. It was cold in his. When he put his arm around her, she pushed him away. "If Matt found us like this, Jim, he'd kill you. He'll be back when he finishes taking care of the horses we rode here."

He thought Terry must be upset and imagining things. He went back to work. "I don't want Big Red up on his feet yet, Terry," he said. "Can you hold his head down?"

"I'll manage, Jim." She had one leg

across the thick neck, holding the horse's head twisted back.

Jim Benton looked up and saw Matt Wagner standing in the lantern light. He felt the man's eyes knife into him. The thin film was no longer visible in the yellow light, and Jim had the uneasy feeling that there was no blindness in the cowman's eyes — that they were steel probes that could read what was in his mind.

Jim was a vet brought here to doctor a sick horse. And if he valued his life, he'd better be damned sure to keep it on that level.

"All set, Terry," Jim Benton said conversationally. "You handle his head, and I'll take care of his hind quarters." Ignoring Matt Wagner's steady stare, Jim continued to inject the warm water and oil. Taking care not to get his head kicked off, he massaged the swollen belly, until he felt the intestines relax.

Jim Benton was blowing as he sat back on his boot heels. He looked up at the bearded cowman, leaning across the door of the box stall. "That does it, mister," he said. "From here on it will be a matter of diet and careful handling, walking him around till the stiffness leaves his joints."

As Jim stood up, he saw the tall shadow

of the cowman move away and leave the barn without saying a word. There was a hundred yards' open clearing from the barn to the house and Jim Benton watched Matt Wagner cover the distance as straight as a man walks a chalk line. Before he had gone twenty feet from the barn, the two big dogs came out of the dugout and trailed him, one on either side.

Jim felt the cold, quick grip of Terry's hand in his as she came to her feet. "I'll take Big Red from here on, Jim," she whispered. "Saddle your horse and for God's sake, get away from here before something happens." There was no mistaking the desperation in her voice.

"I can't leave you alone," Jim said.

"I've been through it alone before. I'll manage."

The big stud wanted up. They helped him to his feet and let him stand until the trembling in his legs was gone. Jim Benton reloaded his saddle bags while Terry held the halter rope.

"Hurry, Jim," she urged. "Saddle your horse and leave."

The crack of a 30-30 put Jim Benton's gun in his hand. The jangling of the cowbell cut through the gun echoes.

"He's at it again, Jim." Terry's breath

caught in a dry sob. "Climb up into the loft. Take your saddle gun and hurry!"

The thought of the two big dogs tearing at his throat sent a shiver down Jim's spine. He slid his carbine from its scabbard and went up the ladder.

The 30-30 cracked a second time and a third. Through the open door Jim could see Matt Wagner against the log wall of the house where he stood with carbine lifted to shoulder level. The clang of the cowbell blended with the sound of each shot. When the shooting stopped, Jim could hear the two big dogs sound a growling, eager whimper that chilled a man's blood.

Terry came up the ladder and dropped the trap door to the stable. "God help us, Jim," she said worriedly. "Those dogs are trained to climb the ladder. They'd tear us both apart unless we shot them first."

"You, too, Terry?"

"Me, too. Both are one-man dogs. And that man is Matt Wagner."

The blind cowman let out a low-toned whistle, like the steam whistle of a locomotive. The four grown pups came charging out of the black maw of the dugout and, snarling and snapping at one another, they ran for the house.

The tall, gaunt cowman took a step out

99

from the wall to put him in the moonlight. His head was tilted to one side as he shoved cartridges into the magazine of the Winchester. "Horsebackers a-comin'," he called out in a quiet, flat-toned voice. "I got the hound pack on the prowl," he added. Then he let out a short laugh.

At the sharp crack of a gun, Terry counted to five, until there were three shots spaced five seconds apart. "That's Chiz at the gate," Terry said.

"Call off them damn dogs, Matt!" Chiz barked in a loud voice.

When the cowman whistled, Jim and Terry watched through the loft door. They saw the big hound pups come loping back. Then Old Chiz rode through the gate toward the house, his saddle gun in his hand.

"Where's Terry? Doc Benton?" he asked Matt Wagner in a saw-filed voice.

"In the barn," Matt answered. His laugh scraped the night.

"Send Duke and Duchess to their hole," Chiz said flatly. "Pronto, Matt."

When Matt gave the signal and the dogs loped toward the dugout, Old Chiz swung from his saddle and the two men went into the house and shut the door. A light showed behind drawn blinds.

"If Big Red don't need walking, we'd better stay up here, Jim," Terry advised. Jim agreed it wasn't worth going down to get torn apart by a pack of savage dogs.

Jim saw Terry silhouetted against the pale light of the door. In her tight-fitting Levi's, she made a cameo outline that quickened his pulse. It was as if Terry had read his innermost thoughts, for she moved back into the shadow.

After a while, Jim cleared his throat and tried to make it casual when he asked, "I just remembered about that big cowbell, Terry. How can Matt hit it from a hundred yards, and him blind?"

"Oh, that," Terry said. "Matt and Chiz rigged the bell and Chiz would stand to one side about fifty feet and pull the rope. At the sound of the bell Matt would shoot. He practiced until he never missed. When Matt shoots at the bell, he stands either at the cabin door or at the barn door," she explained. "He's practiced turning round and round. When he stops, he can point to the north or south or east or west. It's uncanny. Night or day. For Matt Wagner, there is always darkness."

All the time Terry was talking, Jim was staring out the loft door, watching the hounds move restlessly around. He saw

Old Chiz standing at an uncurtained window equipped with heavy shutters.

Terry's conversation was suddenly cut off short by a harsh, indescribable outcry that was neither a scream nor a groan. It was more like the sound of a savage animal caught in a steel trap, excruciating pain mixed with terror, and unlike anything Jim Benton had ever heard. He caught a glimpse of the two big dogs as they raced down the hill, followed by the four big pups.

Jim put an arm around the girl, who was whimpering from fright. He picked up his Winchester and stood there listening and waiting.

The two big dogs kept leaping at the wooden shutters, only to fall back on the ground. The four pups were tangled up in a snarling, fighting pack, fangs bared, close-bunched in a free-for-all dog fight. The fury of the attack built up a horrible din, blotting out any sounds that came from within the cabin.

A couple of the heavy slats tore from the shutters. Seeing the light within seemed to increase the fury of their attack. Then the sound of a .45 and one of the big dogs fell over backwards. When the second dog sprang at the window, the gun spat flame and the dog went down.

They watched Chiz lean through the broken shutter and empty his gun into the snarling pack. He took his time at it, waiting for a sure quick snap shot each time.

Jim kept Terry's face buried in his shoulder so she couldn't see Chiz deliberately shoot the dogs.

"Come a-runnin', Doc." That was Old Chiz's gritty voice.

"Don't go, Jim." Terry's face was chalk white. "Matt's as dangerous as the dogs. He saw us together."

"Matt's blind," Jim reminded her.

"Blind or not, he knows about us. I love you, Jim. If you get yourself killed —"

"Nobody's going to kill me." Jim bent forward and kissed her. "Something has happened at the house. I'll go see what I can do."

Down from the loft, Jim looked the big stud over and told Terry to walk him around for a while. He picked up his saddle bags.

"I'm going to the house with you," Terry said, a stubborn set to her firm little jaw.

Old Chiz, his eyes blue as winter ice, opened the door before they got there. "Matt went out like a light," he told them, as he held the door open for them to go in.

Terry went into the bedroom where Matt lay fully clothed on top of the clean quilt on the bed. She walked to the bedpost where his holstered gun hung. Watching her father's face, she pulled out the gun and backed to the white-washed wall. Her eyes were dangerous as she held the gun in her hand. "Whoever kills Jim Benton won't live to tell about it." She looked at the unconscious man and then at Old Chiz.

Chiz said, "See what you make of it, Doc."

Jim slung his saddle bags over a chair and stepped to the bed. The cowman was tied down with a thick white cotton rope that crossed the back of his neck and over his chest and looped under the bedsprings. Jim cut a quizzical look at Old Chiz.

"When Matt gets one of his spells, he has to be tied down," Chiz explained. "I'd just got him tied in bed when them damned dogs charged."

Jim took the bony wrist in one hand, his watch in the other. Matt's pulse was ragged. Returning his watch to his pocket, Jim asked, "How much whisky has he drunk, Chiz?"

"Hard to say. He was workin' on his

second bottle when it hit him. I saw it comin' and got his gun. He let out a yell, and I had to hit him over the head with his gun barrel before he could grab me around the neck." Old Chiz bared his teeth in a mirthless grin and his eyes slid toward Terry. "Matt had it made to kill Doctor Jim, Terry." He looked at the six-shooter that was too big for her hand.

Terry said nothing, but she shoved the gun back into its holster on the bedpost.

"I'll need a basin and some hot water," Jim Benton said as he rolled his shirt sleeves to the elbow.

When Terry had gone, Old Chiz came over to the bed. He said, "He was goin' to kill you and her both. Claimed he caught you makin' love in the box stall."

"He lied," Jim said firmly. "How the hell could a blind man see a thing like that?"

"You'd be surprised." Chiz's eyes narrowed. "I never knew Matt Wagner to lie about a thing that's important."

Jim's eyes were as cold and hard as those of Old Chiz when he bent over to examine the scalp cut on Matt's head. "That rap was hard enough to cause a concussion," he told Old Chiz. "Possibly a skull fracture. And he's had enough whisky to kill an ordinary man in good health." Jim took the man's wrist again, and felt the uneven pulse. "There's not much a vet can do, except watch him die."

"How about that bullet I told you was lodged against his spinal column?" Old Chiz asked.

"I'm a horse doctor, not a skilled surgeon. He's been to doctors who refused to attempt the removal of that bullet. Either Matt Wagner recovers or he dies, and there isn't anything I can do for the man."

"You sure as hell laid it on the line, Doc."

Terry came in with a clean white towel, a wash basin and a kettle of hot water.

Jim pulled off his soiled shirt and scrubbed his hands and arms. Then he prepared a hypodermic for the sick man. He kept his two fingers on the pulse until it became strong and even. He thumbed back an eyelid and peered into the eye, examining it closely for a long moment.

When Matt's breathing became normal and the color was back in the bearded, gray face, Jim straightened up and told Terry to wash the blood from the scalp wound.

"Can't you do something about the bullet, Jim?" Terry asked, a hopeless desperation in her voice.

Seeing the stricken look in her eyes, Jim said, "Skilled surgeons refused to operate, Terry. If Matt approves, I'll try to do what I can, but I can't promise a thing."

He looked down at the stricken man, whose eyes had opened. "Where's Chiz?" Matt asked weakly.

"Right here, Matt," Chiz answered quickly. "You all right now?"

"I'll manage," said Matt. His eyes never left Jim Benton's face.

"You had a close call, Mister Wagner," Jim said quietly. He let it go at that.

"You was a goner, Matt," Chiz creaked, "until Doc shot some stuff into you. Then you came alive."

"I heard a lot of shooting. I smell burnt powder."

Chiz gave Jim Benton and the girl a warning look. "You went hog wild, Matt," he said. "Shot hell outa things," he lied. "I had to beef you and hogtie you. Doc Benton wants to take a look at that bullet that's lodged against your backbone. Now you're alive, it's up to you to decide."

Matt's eyes opened wider. His big hands clenched until the knuckles whitened. "Have at it, Doc." Chiz loosened the ropes and rolled Matt over on his belly. Matt's voice was muffled when he said, "Cut the damn thing out, Doc. I'd be better off dead than the shape I'm in."

"Have at it, Doc," Chiz said.

Jim Benton reached into the saddle bags and took out a pair of surgical scissors. He cut Matt's shirt from collar to waistband. Then his fingers moved carefully over a lump about the size of a walnut. He said, "Tell me when it hurts."

"I'll let you know," Matt agreed.

The hard lump moved like a marble inside a tight sac of scar tissue. Sweat beaded under Jim's eyes as his finger tips loosened the lead core, moving it from the old adhesions. "That hurt?" he asked in a tight voice.

"Nope. No pain."

"Don't lie," Jim Benton said sharply.

"No pain," Matt repeated. "Feels like somethin's come loose."

Jim motioned for Terry to come around the end of the bed. "Fill a glass full of whisky and put that scalpel in it. Leave it where I can reach it."

Jim was using both hands now to loosen the adhesions that had formed a callus. Kneading the fibrous tissue, the bullet moved half an inch away from the spine and closer to the surface, until it showed like a dark marble under the taut surface of the white skin. Holding it pressed between thumb and forefinger, Jim reached for the scalpel.

"Basin of hot water," he said. "Gauze pads, adhesive, that bottle of alcohol. On the table there where I can reach them." His voice was quiet as he slid the honed edge of the scalpel with a quick smoothness across the taut skin, making a three-inch incision. The bullet rolled out in a trickle of blood.

"That pinched a little," the cowman said in a muffled voice.

Jim let the blood trickle freely, then washed the bullet clean in the hot water and handed it across the bed to Chiz.

Old Chiz let out his breath from behind clenched jaws. "Gawdamighty, Matt." He placed the small hunk of lead in the blind man's hand. "Doc got the job done."

Jim Benton swabbed the open cut with a gauze dressing soaked in an antiseptic solution, then dressed the wound quickly. "Chiz will help get your clothes off," Jim said. "And I want you to stay in bed a day or two. Go light on the booze."

For the first time Jim's hands were unsteady as he rolled a cigarette and went into the kitchen. He gathered up his saddle bags and hat and went out. He had to step around the dead dogs on his way to the barn. Dawn was streaking the gray sky with colors of blood.

All he wanted to do was to get away. Reaction was setting in. The tobacco tasted bitter in his mouth, and he spat the cigarette on the ground and squashed the butt with his boot. The lantern still burned in the barn. He took a quick look at the stud as the horse nickered softly. Anyhow, Big Red was showing thanks in his own way. He was leading his horse from the stall when Terry came into the barn. She was pale and her eyes red-lidded. It had been a hell of a night on the girl as well as on himself.

"Will Dad get back his eyesight?" she asked in a tired voice.

"Matt Wagner," Jim said flatly as he tied on his saddle bags, "has had the partial use of his eyes for quite a while. I don't know just how long," he said wearily, "but that bullet was a quarter of an inch from the spinal column. Chiz could have whittled it out with his jackknife," Jim said, and his voice was bitter.

The sun was two-hours high when he rode up to the Quarantine Station. Speck came out of the barn, a manure fork in his hands. He looked for all the world like an old cowhand, standing hipshot, leaning on the short-handled implement. He had been aping Old Chiz since he was knee high. When he spat through his teeth, Jim Benton wiped the start of a grin from his face.

"What kinda shape was Matt in?" Speck asked.

"He'd been drinking some," Jim said. "Where's Bill Irvin?"

"Gone to round up enough nesters to help with the dippin'," Speck said.

"How about fixing some food to get the wrinkles outa my belly, Speck?"

They went in by the kitchen door. "I'll rustle some grub while you wash up and change into some clean clothes."

Speck did himself proud. Jim told him it was the best breakfast any man ever let out his belt a hole to get around.

"I wish you'd have fetched Terry back with you, Doc."

"Some day, Speck, when my job here is finished, I hope to marry Terry and take her away. We'll want you to come with us wherever we decide to settle down."

He saw the boy's eyes light up, then cloud over. "I'd only be underfoot," Speck said, disappointment in his voice.

"We won't have it otherwise, feller." Jim

111

reached across the table and roughed the kid's hair.

"You asked Terry to marry you, Doc?"

"Yep. She said yes."

"Matt won't let Terry get married, Doc. Ever. To any man. He'll just up and gut shoot you without warnin'."

"Why?" Jim asked bluntly.

"Damned if I know, Doc, for sure I was too young when it happened."

"What happened?" Jim made up his mind to get to the bottom of whatever the mystery was concerning Terry. He had a right to know.

"Like I said, Doc, I was too young to understand. And there's no use askin' Terry."

"Was it something that happened to Terry?"

"No. It happened to her mother."

"Oh." Jim scowled in puzzlement.

"Chiz and Matt are the only ones that know. Chiz is close-mouthed about it, and when Matt gets to broodin', he reaches for the jug. All I know, it was something mighty bad."

"It looks," Jim said slowly as if thinking aloud, "like Terry is paying for whatever her mother did."

"Yeah. It ain't fair," Speck said hotly.

"Makes it tough on Terry," Jim said. "Maybe someday I'll get all of the story."

Jim got up and hung his saddlebags on the buckhorn hatrack. "I'll take five if you'll keep your eyes opened and wake me up if you see anyone coming," Jim said with a yawn.

But bone-tired as he was, sleep wouldn't come, and when it did, it was torn by troubled dreams. Sometime around noon, Speck called to him from outside the open bedroom window.

"Horsebackers comin', Doc. Looks like half a dozen."

Jim Benton pulled on his boots and reached for the field glasses. "Looks like Bill Irvin and five of his nester cowhands," he said aloud.

Jim and Speck were at the barn when the men rode in.

"We loaded our forty years' gatherin's and took the womenfolks and kids in wagons to Bannack," Bill Irvin said. He slapped the wooden stock of his saddle gun. "The Nester Pool is back doin' business. The rest of the men are roundin' up our cattle. We'll have two thousand to dip, so I fetched a few of the boys to help get set up and ready."

"Good," Jim Benton said. "Unsaddle

and turn your horses into the pasture, and we'll get to work."

Bill Irvin and his men dismounted and turned their horses loose. Irvin took Jim aside. "I've got bad news for you, Doc. The stage was held up night before last. We found it abandoned on the old Bannack road while we were movin' our families to town. The six horses had been unharnessed and turned loose. Old Hank Sanford was gut shot, dead by the time we got there."

"Good God!" It was more prayer than blasphemy. Jim Benton's eyes narrowed. That was where Alison McCandless planned to meet the stage at midnight.

"I found this in the boot under the driver's seat." Bill Irvin handed the object to Jim, then walked to where the men waited.

It was Alison's cigarette case. He thumbed the catch. Half a dozen cigarettes with the musk perfume scent were inside. He noticed a thin paper under the cigarettes. He slid it out and unfolded it. He had to examine it closely to make out the hastily penciled words: "In case of my death, I hereby leave and bequeath my share in the Spiderweb Ranch and all live-stock, to Doctor James Benton. Signed,

Alison McCandless. Witnessed, Hank Sanford." Underneath was the date.

It was Alison McCandless' last will and testament, witnessed by a man now dead. Jim read it once more, then replaced it and put the case deep into his pocket, and walked slowly to the house, carrying his own death warrant.

V

It lacked an hour until midnight when Jim Benton sighted the scattered lights of Bannack. The road twisted past the boothill cemetery. As he rode past the fresh mound of dirt that marked the grave of Hank Sanford, Jim took off his hat. There was no prayer in his heart, only a leaden sadness and a wordless prayer.

A strange quiet hung over the town. No horses were tied at the hitchracks, no spurred bootheels on the plank walk. Not even a dog barked at the man who rode along the dusty street.

Sitting straight in the saddle, Jim Benton had the uncomfortable feeling of being watched by unseen eyes. He was glad when he reached the White Elephant Feed and Livery Stable at the end of the street. The barn doors were open and the lantern hanging on the end of a rope shed a shadowy glow over the box stalls.

Jim Benton dismounted and led his horse into an empty stall. There was no barn man around, so he picked up a halter rope and tied it around his horse's neck and slid off the headstall and hung it across the saddle horn. As he was graining his horse, another horse in the adjoining stall nickered softly and he let the animal nibble at the can of oats in his hand. Even in the dim light he knew the black thoroughbred filly belonged to Alison McCandless.

As he came out of the box stall with the empty grain can, he caught sight of the short, stocky man in the double doorway of the stable. There was something stolidly menacing about the way he stood, his bowed legs spread apart, his hat slanting down across one eye. He was a squat, barrel-chested, heavy-shouldered man with a battered-looking face. He was twirling a short, thick club which left his hand, spun upward and flipped over once before the man grabbed it out of midair. There was a gnarled knot on the business end of the club. A nickel-plated star pinned to an unbuttoned vest shone in the lamplight.

"Now who the hell may you be, gawkin' at other people's horses?" He talked like a man with a chip on his shoulder.

"I'm Jim Benton from the Quarantine Station on Grasshopper," Jim answered. "I came to town to talk to Judge Bryan."

The squat little Irishman gestured with his club and said, "I'm Barney Kelly, Town Marshal of Bannack. Owner of this stable. Come along and I'll walk ye up the street to the Bannack Hotel. His Honor is upstairs in his private chambers."

"About that black filly —" Jim didn't finish before the Marshal interrupted.

"The filly was in the stall early one mornin'. That's all I know." There was a finality to the husky voice that forbade questioning.

As they walked up the street, Jim took notice of a wide band of black crepe stitched to the sleeve of Kelly's rusty black coat.

Jim Benton indicated the badge of mourning. "Hank Sanford?" he asked.

"May his soul rest in peace." Barney Kelly crossed himself.

They went to the desk in the small hotel lobby. Barney said, "He says his name is Jim Benton. Wants to talk to Judge Bryan. Upstairs." Barney motioned with his club.

He tapped gently with the Irish shillalah on the closed door, then opened it and stood aside for Jim Benton to enter.

A tall man in black broadcloth sat in a swivel chair at his desk. His hair was thick and white, the white beard and mustache carefully trimmed, his features bold-chiseled.

In the silence Jim Benton saw the ice thaw in the man's eyes, the smile erasing the stern lines of the granite mask. He put down the pen and got to his feet, his hand extended in welcome. "You are Dr. Hugh Benton's son. I know without being told. I'm the lad's godfather, Barney," he said. The Marshal went downstairs.

"The cold-blooded killing of Hank Sanford," Judge Bryan explained, "has Bannack up in arms. Nobody trusts a stranger, and if Lorne Mackin or any Spiderweb cowhand should ride into town, there would be a lynching." Judge Bryan waved his guest into a big armchair.

"I should have come to Bannack before now to pay my respects, sir."

"From what I hear," the judge said, "Jim Benton has been a busy man. My guess is that you are in town now for a purpose."

"Yes, sir." Jim took the silver cigarette case from his pocket. "This belongs to Alison McCandless," he explained. "She was supposed to be on the stage when Hank Sanford was murdered. This was found in the stage and given to me." Jim removed the onion skin paper and handed it to the Judge. "This is Alison's will, witnessed by Hank Sanford."

Judge Bryan hooked a pair of steel-rimmed spectacles behind his ears. "Both signatures seem to be genuine. I've known Hank Sanford's scrawl for years and I have handled Alison McCandless' legal affairs for the past year." He tapped the flimsy paper with a fingernail. "This last will, if submitted in probate court, will stand on its own merits." He folded the paper and put it back in the case, snapping it shut. He looked at the younger man with a speculative glance.

"I don't want any part of the Spiderweb outfit," Jim Benton said quickly. "I wouldn't touch it with a prod pole. I can't tell you any more than that, sir." Jim squirmed uncomfortably.

"I understand, Jim." Judge Bryan smiled a little. "Take it easy. You're not on the witness stand." Then he added, "I advised Alison McCandless to leave her husband. Cass is a ruthless man. Married to a beautiful girl young enough to be his daughter, he was jealous and suspicious."

Jim Benton felt his face get hot. "I guess McCandless had a right to be jealous," he said, trying to sound indifferent. Now that he had an opening wedge, he told the Judge as much and as little of Alison and himself without going into details. He was glad enough to get it off his mind.

"Alison McCandless is a remarkable woman," Judge Bryan said. "Beautiful and cold as a marble statue. Dangerous as a white flame. Mercenary enough to sell herself to Cass McCandless. Later, when she realized the big Texan's brutality, she wanted out." He turned the cigarette case over in his hands. "I'm keeping this. But I have reason to believe that Alison McCandless is alive."

"Then she did ride the black filly I saw in the barn," Jim Benton said coldly. "Alison is alive. Hank Sanford is dead. His blood's on her lily-white hands," he finished bitterly.

Judge Bryan shook his leonine head. "I'm sure Alison McCandless had nothing to do with Hank Sanford's murder. I am betraying no secret when I tell you that Hank was once a member of the Vigilantes," he said evenly.

"Whoever killed him and left him hanging to the hangman's tree in Bannack took time out to pin a sheet of torn wrapping paper to his shirt. The numbers 3-7-77 were printed on the paper. It's the old Vigilante warning."

A hard-knuckled rap sounded on the

door. Without waiting for the summons to enter, the knob turned and the door opened. A rangy, six foot five man, under a high-crowned black Stetson, stooped to get through the door. He stepped inside and kicked the door shut behind him. His long-jawed, hook-nosed face was cadaverous. Black brows tufted in an ugly scowl, meeting in the deep crease over the high-bridged beak. Pale eyes were set deep in dark sockets, the mouth a knife slash under a short upper lip. His face was taut rawhide stretched across the bony structure.

"It's been a long time, Judge. You remember me?"

"I know you," Judge Bryan said coldly.

"Igo," the man spat it across the room as he palmed a law badge for the two men to see. "Stock Inspector. I'm back in Montana to stay." As John Igo's slivered eyes watched both men, he opened the door and left the room.

Judge Bryan's gaze was fixed on the closed door. He had the look of a man who had just seen a ghost. And Igo had the look of a man who had just come back from hell. With a visible effort Judge Bryan turned his eyes from the door to the top drawer of his desk and took out a small black leather book. He cleared his throat and his quiet voice fell across the silent room. "Since I came West in '61, I have kept a diary," he said with effort.

"December 24th, 1863," he read aloud. "Seven men, known members of the Henry Plummer Gang, were tried by the Vigilantes and sentenced to hang. The execution was duly carried out at the hangman's tree at the Bannack Stage Station. The seven outlaws and one other man, a boy of seventeen, were captured at Robbers Roost, but the week before their arrest one of the outlaws awakened Dr. Benton at midnight and told him to board the stage with his medical kit. He was needed to attend the wounds of the youngest member of the Plummer Gang. Under the threat of death at gunpoint, he was sworn to secrecy.

"When the stage pulled out, it was stopped by armed men, and Hank Sanford, the driver, was told to drive off on a side road leading to the Roost. With a grim warning Hank Sanford was later allowed to go on his way, with the promise to stop on his return trip to pick up Dr. Hugh Benton."

A faraway look crept into the old Judge's eyes, as he stared across the room.

Jim Benton cleared his throat and started to rise.

"Listen to the rest of it, Jim," the Judge said. "Neither Dr. Benton nor Hank Sanford ever betrayed in any way the presence of the outlaws at Robbers Roost, but the following week when the eight outlaws were captured, the wounded outlaw, the youngest one, accused Hank and the doctor of violating their sworn word. His accusations were bitter, but unfounded and unjust.

"On account of the young outlaw's age, he was not sentenced to hang with the others. Instead, Dr. Hugh Benton suggested that he be turned loose with the Vigilante written notice handed to him, which gave him three hours, seven minutes and seventy-seven seconds to quit Montana and never return under penalty of death. The cabalistic warning numbers were written by the doctor, a member of the Vigilantes, on a sheet of paper torn from his prescription pad."

Judge Bryan closed the book and put it back in the drawer. "You have just seen that young outlaw grown to manhood. His name is John Igo," Judge Bryan said quietly. "Somewhere Igo has served a long prison term. It's stamped on his face. But in returning to Montana, Igo has violated the terms set down by the Vigilantes, and I intend to have him brought before the Supreme Court if it is my last judicial act on earth. It will be a very interesting test case to see if the State of Montana will uphold the banishment."

Jim Benton listened while the Judge talked of pioneer days and his friendship with Jim's father. When he had finished, Jim said he would have to be getting back to the Quarantine Station.

"Watch out for that renegade, Igo," Judge Bryan warned him as they shook hands.

Later, when Jim Benton rode out of town, his thoughts went back to the time his father was alive. He was deep in his musings when the tall horseman rode out to block his way. He had a gun in his hand.

"Your old man was Doctor Hugh Benton," Igo said flatly. "Time me'n' you had a confidential. You're the government man in charge of the quarantine. I'm the Stock Inspector. Lorne Mackin, the Spiderweb ramrod, is at Sundown. That's where me'n' you are headed."

"Suits me fine," Jim Benton said coldly. "You don't need that gun," he added contemptuously.

Jim Benton offered no comment when John Igo reined his horse to take the old stage road. When there was no longer danger of Indian attacks and after the Vigilantes had rid Montana Territory of the Plummer Gang, the old stage road to Bannack had been abandoned. Windblown sand covered the ruts, and grass and tall weeds grew rank. But Hank Sanford had used the old wagon road to go five or six miles out of his way to pick up Alison McCandless at the abandoned station, and it had cost him his life. Riding straight-backed in his saddle, with his hat slanted across his eyes, Igo neither looked at nor spoke to Jim Benton. And there was something about the tall man's brooding silence that forbade questioning. It was as if the man rode alone, wrapping the silence around him like a blanket.

Igo led him to a group of sod-roofed, log buildings, long deserted. A short distance away stood a large, old cottonwood that had been struck by lightning. Dead limbs showed like skeleton arms, with bony, fleshless fingers bent and clawing at the night.

Igo reined up under the tree. "I once watched seven friends hang from this tree," he said in a lifeless tone. "I sat my horse, waiting my turn, when one of the Vigilantes rode up alongside me. He handed me a slip of paper with the numbers 3-7-77 written on it. He told me I had three hours, seven minutes, and seventy-seven seconds to quit Montana and never return. That man was Doctor Hugh Benton." Without another word, the tall, lean man in black, reined his horse and rode away at a running walk.

Jim Benton followed the Stock Inspector, who lifted his horse to a long trot on the short cut to Sundown.

The only light in the deserted, ravaged town came from the Longhorn Saloon. The sickly glow that showed above the swinging half-doors revealed the shambles inside of what had once been the most ornate and elaborate saloon in that part of the cow country.

It was the prideful boast of the Cattle King from the Texas Panhandle that he owned the town of Sundown. If so, his Spiderweb outfit had fouled their own nest.

Sitting his saddle at the deserted hitch-rack, Jim Benton watched Igo shoulder through the swinging doors, his hand on his gun. Broken glass crunched as Igo crossed the littered floor to the bar. He prowled around until he found a sealed bottle of whisky and, tipping it, he drank a long drink.

"Stand your hand, Benton!"

The flat voice made a soundless echo along the deserted street. Twisting around in the saddle, Jim Benton shifted his weight to one stirrup. The voice had come from a bedroom window in the hotel, the bridal suite that Alison McCandless had fled from when she slid down one of the posts that supported the wooden awning.

"We need a doctor up here," the voice said. "Hurry it up, Benton."

Igo vaulted the bar, his gun in his hand, as he peered over the swinging half-doors. "What goes on, Benton?"

The sound of the man's laugh from behind the blind on the bedroom window was barbed. "Back up, Igo," he warned. "Step outside and you'll get a bellyful of lead for breakfast. Get back to your bottle."

"You got the deal, Skeeter," Igo called back. "But one thing. Benton comes back down here alive. Anything happens to him, you and Mackin will wind up in hell's hot acre."

Jim Benton dismounted and dropped his

bridle reins across the hitchrack. "Do what he says, Igo. I can take my own part," Jim said gruffly. He turned and walked across the street. If Alison was up there and hurt badly enough to need medical care, he told himself, somebody was going to pay for it, and he didn't need Igo to back his hand.

The wizened-looking Skeeter was waiting for him in the upper hallway. He noticed that Jim's hand was on the butt of his gun. "No need for gun play, Benton. We need a doc. If we needed a gunslinger, I'd have called Igo." Skeeter shoved open a door and stood aside.

"Go ahead, Skeeter," Jim Benton said bluntly. "I don't want a knife in my gizzard."

Skeeter let out a cackling sound and went into the room. He turned up the wick of the lamp on a table near the bed, where Lorne Mackin sat propped up with pillows. He was naked to the waist.

"Shut the door, Skeeter, and let Benton take a look," Mackin said. He turned pain-seared eyes toward Benton. "That bitch McCandless married blasted the door with buckshot, and I stopped some of it. I tried to pick it out of my belly, but it's too deep."

Jim noticed the blood-flecked bandage

around Mackin's middle. "How long you been in bed, Mackin?" Jim asked, eyeing the man with cold suspicion.

"Since I crawled into it, the night that bitch peppered me."

Jim Benton rolled up his shirt-sleeves. He cut a look at Skeeter crouched down by the window, Winchester across his knees.

"I got to keep an eye out for Igo," Skeeter said when he saw Jim looking at him. "If you need anything, holler down to the Chink in the kitchen. Your doctor's bag and saddlebags are in that gunnysack in the corner."

"I sent a couple of the boys to the Quarantine Station," Lorne Mackin cut in. "You wasn't there, so they brought your stuff and left word at the Nester Pool camp where you could find it."

Jim choked back the hot anger inside him. It was a while before he could trust his voice. "I'll make a deal with you, Mackin," he said. "I'll do what I can to patch you up, providing you get word to your boys to gather all the Spiderweb cattle and hold them ready for dipping."

"It's a deal, Benton. Get to work."

Jim Benton cut the dirty bandages loose. When he peeled them off from the tender hairy skin, Lorne Mackin gritted back a shrill outcry as they ripped free. "God-damn, you're rougher than a butcher!"

"You better start showing that toughness you brag about, Mackin," Jim said. He took what looked like a steel toothpick from his bag and held it up so the wounded man could get a good look at it. "When I start fishing for the buckshot with this probe, it's going to hurt. One nervous jerk and this pick could puncture your intestines, and it would be all over but the lily in your hand."

Jim noticed an old scar on Mackin's lower rib and ran his thumb down its four-inch length. He was recalling something that Alison had said about shooting the Spiderweb ramrod with a pistol. "That was a close miss. Who gave you that, Mackin?" Jim asked.

The wounded man's teeth bared, his eyes murderous. Skeeter cackled thinly. Then the Chinaman padded in with a big kettle of hot water Jim had wanted.

Jim was busy for several minutes cleaning the abdomen. When he finished, he looked down into the yellowed, sweat-beaded face, and said, "So far as I can see there are half a dozen buckshot deeply embedded. It's going to be painful as hell probing for them. I can put you to sleep with chloroform, and in a half hour the job will be over."

"What's to keep you from puttin' me to sleep for keeps, Benton?"

"To go to sleep and never wake up would be too easy for you, Mackin." A lopsided grin spread his wide mouth. "I'd be cheating the gallows. I hope to see you and Skeeter Owens strung up from the same tree limb for the murder of Hank Sanford."

"I had nothing to do with it!" Lorne Mackin said savagely. "I was laid up right here in this bed. Skeeter was here with me."

"The murder was done by your Spiderweb gunslingers, Mackin. You're the ramrod who gave them their orders."

"I never gave no such orders, Benton. If the Spiderweb hired hands did it, they were strictly on their own. You got my word for it. Take it or leave it lay."

For some reason Jim Benton got the idea Mackin was telling the truth. He held up the chloroform can. "Make it easy on yourself, Mackin."

"Have at it. I couldn't stand watchin' you stick that spike into my belly."

"You'll be back on your feet tomorrow. Get your Spiderweb cattle rounded up and held ready to dip next week."

"It's a deal, Benton."

Jim held the saturated gauze over his nose.

A minute later he lifted the pad and checked the pulse. Then he went to work with the steel probe. One by one he put the lead pellets into a clean ash tray and swabbed the blood away. When he finished the job, he covered Mackin with the sheet and rolled his own shirt-sleeves down. "Chances are, Skeeter," he said, "Mackin will wake up sick as a poisoned pup, but he'll be able to ride in a couple of days."

"I'll shore know where to come if I ever get shot up, Doc."

Jim Benton's eyes pinned the scrawny cowhand to the wall. "Where's Cass McCandless' wife, Skeeter?" he asked.

"You got me there, Doc. Last time I saw her she was ridin' out of town. I figured you had her on ice somewhere."

Jim Benton didn't think Skeeter was lying. He put on his hat and hitched up his cartridge belt. "What's to keep you from shooting me in the back when I leave here?" he asked coldly.

"Igo," Skeeter replied waspishly. "A bounty hunter called John Igo. He gave me the slip while I watched you work on

133

Mackin." He pulled the blind to one side. Both horses were gone from the hitchrack. "Matt Wagner's boy rode into town while you was pickin' that buckshot out of Lorne. I let him lead your horse to the livery stable. Like as not he's waitin' there for you."

"You let Speck get away?"

"I don't shoot kids, Benton."

Jim Benton picked up his black bag and the saddlebags. When he opened the door, John Igo was standing in the shadowed hallway with a gun in his hand.

"I'll cover you, Benton." He jerked his head sideways. "Matt Wagner's kid is waitin' at the barn. Get goin'. A man can crowd his luck too far."

Skeeter cackled dryly as he came to the door. "Me'n' Igo's got a workin' agreement, Doc," he said. "Mackin agreed to gather the Spiderweb cattle. We'll see to it he keeps his end of the deal. You kept yours. But like Igo says, don't crowd your luck too far."

Jim Benton found Speck waiting at the barn. He gripped his shoulder and said, "You'll do to take along, feller. Let's get goin'."

After Jim Benton and Speck had eaten a

late breakfast, they caught fresh horses from the Pool remuda and rode out to the two big cattle herds.

"We'll cull everything that shows any sign of the Texas Tick fever, Bill," Jim told the Pool ramrod.

Irvin gave his men their orders, and when they had finished culling the herd at noon, there was about two hundred and fifty head in the cut. Irvin left enough men to hold the cattle and the rest of them rode to camp for noon dinner and a change of horses.

Jim Benton sensed the cool attitude of the Pool wagon boss and his men. "Something stuck in your craw, Bill?" He came to the point without any preamble as the two rode to camp together.

"The government wants all cattle showing signs of tick fever destroyed," Bill Irvin said. "Out of the cattle we just culled, there's about fifty ga'nted up and slobberin'. The rest are only in fair-to-middlin' shape." Bill Irvin looked straight at Jim, and said, "The Pool men are none too happy about killin' off cattle that might make a live of it. You're in charge, Doc. The Pool men said to tell you how they felt about it."

"I figured that was the grievance, Bill,"

Jim Benton said quietly. "But I have my orders. I'm just a hired man working for Uncle Sam."

"Every man in the Nester Pool is on the rocks," Bill Irvin said. "McCandless grabbed our ranches, run us off our land, and all we got left are those cattle. If Uncle Sam would pay us for the ticky cattle we kill, it would make a different story. As things stand, the Nester Pool has a belly-ache."

"To hell with government red tape, Bill," Jim Benton said, a slow grin spreading his homely face. "We'll destroy only the fifty head, dip the rest, and hold them in feed lots. Shovel Uncle Sam's hay into them and continue the dipping until the cattle are tick free and healthy. Then we'll dip the tick free cattle and turn them into government pasture."

"Ain't you kinda stickin' your neck out, Doc?"

"It's my neck, Bill. I've got the right to shove it out as far as it'll stretch. There's no need for you Nester Pool fellers to advertise it, however."

"I'll tell the men."

"The Spiderweb's dipping their cattle, Bill," Jim said carelessly.

"Uh!" Irvin grunted.

136

When Jim had finished telling Irvin about the deal with Mackin, Irvin said, "I'll be damned. Cass McCandless is goin' to blow up when he gets the news."

"McCandless is somewhere in Texas. The job will be done before he knows about it, I hope," Jim said, shifting his weight to one stirrup. "As near as I could get a count, Bill," he said, "you're holding a hundred head of Spiderweb cattle in your day herd."

The incredulous half-grin that had formed about Bill Irvin's mouth at the news quickly disappeared, leaving his eyes cold. "One hundred and thirty-seven by actual tally, Doc. All of them cattle the brand artist, Skeeter Owens, worked from the Pool brands into the Spiderweb. We'll cut and hold them till the Stock Inspector shows up. Slim Smith tells me a John Igo has been appointed to the job."

"That's right, Bill," Jim said darkly.

As they rode into camp, swung down and unsaddled, Jim Benton caught sight of Speck behind the mess tent where he was making frantic motions, pointing at the tent. Before he could puzzle it out, John Igo stepped out of the tent, a cup of coffee in his hand and a half-smoked cigarette hanging from a corner of his mouth.

Igo took a stiff-legged step to bar Bill Irvin's way into the mess tent. "You ramroddin' this outfit?" he asked, staring down at the short, stocky Irvin.

"That's right," Bill said quietly.

"I'm John Igo, Stock Inspector. I understand you got some Spiderweb cattle in your day herd. Get rid of them or I'll hold the herd up for a Winchester cut."

The Pool wagon boss stood with his legs spread, the fringed shotgun chaps saddle-warped to his bowed legs. His voice was saw-edged when he said, "Them Spiderweb cattle belong to the Nester Pool cowmen. They were picked up as calves and the brands worked into the Spiderweb by a brand artist named Skeeter Owens."

"The law reads," Igo said in a toneless voice, "that you got to catch a brand artist red-handed. I'd go slow accusing Skeeter of brand changing."

"I'm a paid-up member of the Stockgrowers' Association that hired you, Igo," Irvin said hotly. "Go easy on that talk about a Winchester cut."

"Cut the cattle out," Igo snapped. "Pen them at the Quarantine Station corrals. I'll look them over." He motioned to Jim Benton with his head. "Let's me'n' you have a talk, Benton." He walked away.

"What's on your mind, Igo?" Jim asked, when he caught up with him.

The Stock Inspector took his time to answer. Then he removed a flat wallet from his pants pocket and held it palmed in his hand. "When the Vigilantes hung Big Nose George Curry to a telegraph pole at Rawlins," Igo said in a flat voice, "they skinned his tough hide and tanned it, and made it into leather goods. Some of them as souvenirs. This is all I got left to remind me of Big Nose George."

Igo turned the wallet over, the ghost of a smile twitching his lipless mouth. From the wallet he took out a folded paper, yellowed with age, and sliding the wallet back into his pocket, he handed the paper to Jim Benton.

"Your old man handed this to me when he ordered me to leave Montana," Igo explained. "Here, take it. I'm giving his son the same deal. Get the hell out of the country, Benton."

As Igo swung into the saddle and rode away, Jim Benton unfolded the old prescription blank with the Vigilante warning numbers, 3-7-77, written on it.

By mid-afternoon the cattle in the disputed Spiderweb brand were penned in the corral at the Quarantine Station. After an hour's waiting around, there was no sign of the Stock Inspector.

"Don't look like Igo's goin' to show up, Doc." The Nester Pool wagon boss broke the uneasy silence.

"I had a hunch Igo wouldn't put in his official appearance." Jim Benton tried to keep the relief in his voice from showing.

"How come, Doc?" Irvin asked bluntly.

"Igo hasn't a leg to stand on when he rides through the government gate. This land belongs to Uncle Sam, and I'm the boss here."

When Igo didn't show up in another hour, Jim Benton told Bill Irvin to send word out to the men on day herd. All Nester Pool cattle were to be shoved through the gate and bedded down inside the government fence. "Igo had a mean eye when he left camp," Jim said. "I wouldn't put it past him to stampede your cattle."

"Remind me some evenin', Doc, to whittle you out a leather medal," Irvin said.

When the cattle were bedded down and two men left on guard, Jim Benton and Speck ate supper at the Pool mess wagon down the creek. After supper they rode back to the Quarantine Station and stabled their horses.

Sometime during the night Jim came wide awake and sat up with his gun in his hand. The tapping sound on the window pane had awakened him. His first thought was of John Igo. Tapping on a man's window to get him to look out was a time-worn bushwhacker's trick.

"Jim," the voice was muffled. "It's Terry. Open the window."

It could be a gun trap with Terry for bait. He crept his way cautiously in sock feet to the window. Standing back along the wall, he reached out and released the catch, opened the window, and raised the shade. He waited. The next moment Terry Wagner climbed through the window. Jim lowered the window, fastening it securely, and pulled the shade.

"Why the midnight visit, Terry?" he asked.

"Chiz came with me. We fetched some horses. I put Big Red in a stall. Chiz pastured the horses, and then pulled out."

"Where is your father?"

"Gone. He rode away last night. Chiz said I was to stay here."

"What happened after I left, Terry?"

"Nothing much. Dad quieted down and slept off the whisky. When he awoke, he dressed and prowled around with his gun.

Then a stranger rode up about supper time. He was a hard-looking character I'd never seen before," she said quietly. "I heard him tell Dad and Chiz he'd come from Bannack and that a man named John Igo had been appointed Stock Inspector by the Stockgrowers' Association and that he was on the prowl." Terry handed Jim a package. "He brought this. Said to give it to you."

Jim took the package. It was addressed to him from Dr. Roscoe Spencer at Hamilton. "This is vaccine for Rocky Mountain Spotted Fever," he said. "How did this tough character get hold of it?"

"I don't know, Jim. I heard him say he'd found it in the stage coach, and that old Hank Sanford had been murdered."

Jim fixed Terry a bed in the front room, then went back to his own bunk. When he had stretched out, he remembered the package and got up and lit the lamp again. There was a sealed envelope stuck in the string of the package. It bore no name or address, and as Jim held it up to the light a strange premonition of disaster tightened his belly. His fingers were a little unsteady as he pulled out a single sheet of folded paper.

Jim read: "This is to inform you of the hanging of Judge Bryan in his rooms at the Bannack Hotel." It was initialed A.

VI

Jim Benton moved like a sleepwalker in the early dawn. As he reached the barn, a man stepped out into the gray light, a Winchester in the crook of his arm. Jim reached for his six-shooter.

"Hold it, Benton!" The man's voice was scratchy.

Jim recognized Barney Kelly, the owner of the livery stable and the Town Marshal of Bannack.

"Judge Bryan," Kelly said, "is in a bad way."

"Hanged," Jim Benton replied. "Where were you and your tin star while they were lynching the Judge?" he asked, his voice cold with fury.

"There was no public lynching, Benton. It was a strictly private affair. Strung him up in his rooms in the wee small hours. By the Grace of God, he was cut down in time." He crossed himself hastily.

"You mean," Jim Benton said dazedly, "Judge Bryan is alive?"

"If you can call it that."

"Who's looking after him?"

"Cass McCandless' young wife. It was her who cut him down. She sent me to fetch you, Doc. How soon can you be ready?"

"Right now. I'll get my satchel from the house." He paused, scowling thoughtfully for a long moment. "I'm taking Terry Wagner and young Speck with me to Bannack. They'll be a lot safer in town than here."

Terry had a clean floursack apron tied on and was getting breakfast when Jim entered the kitchen.

"I'm making a hurry-up trip to Bannack, Terry, and I'm taking you and Speck with me. I'll tell you about it as we ride to town."

"The coffee's ready. I'll have breakfast on the table in a jiffy," Terry said.

"You and Speck grab something to eat. I'll settle for coffee. Judge Bryan was hanged in his room at the hotel. He was cut down in time but he may be dead by the time I get to Bannack," Jim told her so that she would hurry.

Terry's hands were unsteady as she poured the coffee. "Who was that man you were talking to at the barn, Jim?"

"Barney Kelly. Town Marshal at Bannack."

"Is he looking for Matt Wagner?"

"Not that I know of. Why should he, Terry?"

"To arrest him," she said, trying to keep her voice steady, "for hanging Judge Bryan."

When Terry saw the surprised look on Jim Benton's face, she added, "It goes back to when I was in pigtails. I meant to tell you about it before. My mother ran away from Matt and took me with her to Bannack. He followed us and Judge Bryan heard him using abusive language to my mother in the hotel dining room. He came over to our table where Matt was standing, ugly drunk. He told Matt he was Judge Bryan, known as the Hanging Judge of Bannack. He ordered my father out of town and told him to stay away, that he was taking his wife and child into the protective custody of the law. We stayed at the Bryan home. Day and night Matt kept sending threats by any cowpuncher headed for Bannack. We lived in constant fear. When word reached Bannack that there had been a gun battle with the Spiderweb outfit and that Matt Wagner was dying, Mama told Judge Bryan that she was going back to look after Matt. From that time on, until she died, Mama's life was hell on earth. Matt still held a grudge against the Judge that he intended to settle someday. It was Matt who hung Judge Bryan, Jim," Terry finished.

Jim Benton had nothing to say. He had seen enough of the man to realize he was capable of the crime.

"I have to give Irvin a few instructions," Jim said, as he finished the coffee, and picked up his bag. "No sense in eating your heart out, Terry," he said kindly. "Judge Bryan has a chance to live and he'll need you to look after him."

On the ride to Bannack, Jim Benton and Terry were in the lead. Speck and Barney followed behind, and Speck's laughter told them that he had forgotten that Barney had a star pinned to his vest.

"Barney has a way with horses," Terry said, as she rode beside Jim. "I'm giving him Big Red. He'll have a good home and there'll be no Matt Wagner to stand at a safe distance to curse and crack a bull-whip." There was a quaver in her voice, as she continued. "Matt tried to poison Big Red. He murdered the man who saw him put the arsenic into Big Red's grain. That was all a lie Matt made up. He told me about it."

"A man don't confess to a brutal crime

like that without reason."

"Matt Wagner has his reason. According to his drunken way of thinking, he was punishing me. When I told Chiz about it, he had it out with Matt. Matt saddled up. I watched him ride away and I don't care if I never see him again.

Jim Benton and Terry Wagner dismounted in front of the hotel, while Barney Kelly and Speck rode to the stable.

When they entered the Judge's rooms, Jim Benton expected to see Alison McCandless. But it was Bill Irvin's wife who was caring for the sick man.

"Alison has gone." Mrs. Irvin answered the question in Jim's eyes. "She left me in charge."

Nervous and unsure of himself, Jim Benton looked down at Judge Bryan. He had the appearance of a dying man, his eyes fixed with an unwinking stare at the ceiling. The pulse was feeble.

Jim peeled off his dust-grimed shirt and began washing. Then he busied himself preparing a heart stimulant for the old Judge. After he had given the injection, a little color seemed to come through the gray pallor and the bearded lips were no longer blue.

He eased both his hands under the injured neck, his fingers working gently along the spinal column until he eased the vertebra back into place. The injured man's eyes were squinted shut. Pain had driven the blood from his face. "That hurt like hell, Judge, and I'm sorry," Jim Benton apologized. He gave the sick man an injection of morphine to ease the pain and to let him sleep.

Jim remembered how his father had rigged up a neck brace for a bronc rider who had gotten bucked off, dislocating a vertebra. The bronc rider had called it a horse collar. Jim would find the saddle shop and see what he could rig up.

In the room Judge Bryan used for an office, Jim found Terry and Mrs. Irvin. The nester's wife said she wanted to take Terry to the Mercantile and get her some feminine clothes. "All she's ever worn is Levi's. I can hardly wait till I see her in a dress."

"I'll get the proprietor to sit in the bedroom for an hour," Jim said. "You two do some shopping." He pulled out a wad of crumpled money and handed it to Terry. "While you're in the store, buy a corset with whalebone ribs. Fetch it to the saddle shop."

Terry winked slyly at the older woman, and said, "What size do you think I'll take, Dr. Benton?"

Jim Benton's face reddened with embarrassment. "I want the whalebone stays to rig up a leather brace for Judge Bryan's neck," he explained.

As soon as the hotel man came up, Jim went downstairs to the bar. Barney Kelly stood at the far end of the bar with Speck, who was drinking a bottle of pop. Men lined the bar, shoulder to shoulder. Their talk broke off when he came in. Every man was looking at Jim's reflection in the long mirror behind the back bar.

Something about the hushed silence and the looks of cold suspicion warned Jim Benton in advance. Standing with his foot on the brass rail was a six-foot, heavy-shouldered man. On each side of him were two tough-looking characters.

"Sundowners," came Speck's sibilant whisper as he edged up alongside Jim.

"Get up to Judge Bryan's room, feller," Jim Benton told Speck. "Pronto." He had seen the big cowpuncher down his drink and step away from the bar, his two companions following. Dragging his spur rowels through the sawdust on the floor, the big man blocked Jim Benton's

149

way to the bar.

"You the big dawg with the brass collar in charge of the Quarantine Station?" he asked sarcastically.

"I'm the man." Jim Benton tried to hold his temper. "If you lost a big dog with a brass collar, you better go back to Sundown and whistle."

The man ignored the remark. He said, "There's three thousand head of Spiderweb cattle crowdin' your fence, but no government man there to handle the dippin'. What about it, Benton?"

"The Nester Pool outfit is dipping today," Jim said, watching the big man narrowly. "Tell Lorne Mackin it will be the day after tomorrow before I can refill the vat and dip his cattle."

An ugly grin spread across the big man's battered face. "Lorne Mackin ain't ramroddin' this Spiderweb roundup. Him and Skeeter Owens drifted yonderly."

"All right." Jim Benton eyed him suspiciously. "Then take word to whoever's ramroddin' the Spiderweb outfit."

"You're lookin' at him, Benton. Pecos Johnson. One of the Johnson Boys. From Tascosa in the Texas Panhandle."

"Then hold your herd back," Jim Benton said, "till I send you word to tally them

150

through the gate."

The big cowpuncher hitched up his sagging cartridge belt. He said with a sideways grin, "I take my orders from only one man. His name is Cass McCandless." He tongued the big wad of chewing tobacco that bulged his cheek, then spat a brown stream into the damp sawdust between Jim's boots. "The Spiderweb cattle go through the gate at daybreak tomorrow morning." His mouth twisted into a lewd grin. "Lorne Mackin told me if you wasn't at the Quarantine Station, I'd find you somewhere smellin' around McCandless' pretty young wife." His hand closed over the butt of his holstered gun.

Jim Benton moved without warning. His right fist hit the man's belly, sinking wrist deep. Timed to the split second, it was a paralyzing solar plexus punch, delivered with the science of the prize ring.

The drawn gun slid from the big man's hand as he jackknifed. Jim Benton's left caught his jaw as he went down. The uppercut snapped his head back. His knees hinged and buckled. Jim sidestepped the fall. His looping swing caught a second man below the waistband. It was a foul blow, meant to be that way. The man groaned and doubled up. He dropped his gun and grabbed himself with both hands.

Barney Kelly moved in fast. He slapped the gun from the third man's hand as he pulled it from the holster. Barney's huge fist hit the man square in the face. Blood spurted from the smashed nose. His second punch was a haymaker that hit the point of the jaw, lifting the man off his feet. He was out like a light when he landed on his back.

Speck came in whistling soundlessly. "I set them three Spiderweb Sundowners afoot," he said, jerking a thumb toward the outside. "Untied their horses at the hitch rack and led them around into the alley." He looked down at the three motionless cowhands. "Gosh, Doc," he said, "when you and Barney hit a man, they stay hit."

Jim turned to Barney Kelly. "Where's the saddle shop, Barney?" he asked.

"Next door to the barber shop. I'll take you there." Barney went in behind the bar and came out with a pail filled with water. He dumped it on the big man's head. When he came to life, Barney told him, "Pick yourself up and get out of town. Take your two pals with you." Kelly collected their guns and handed them across the bar. He kicked the other men onto their feet. "If ever any of you show up in

Bannack again, there'll be a necktie party."

Jim Benton told the big cowpuncher who was swaying on his feet, "Keep your Spiderweb cattle clear of the Quarantine Station until I send you word. It might be day after tomorrow or a week from then. Your horses are tied up in the alley. Get going."

When the three men staggered out and rode away, Jim Benton and Barney Kelly walked down the street in silence. Barney unlocked the saddle shop door and they went in. Inside, Barney gave Jim Benton a letter. He said, "Alison McCandless told me to give this to you, before she rode away. I've kept the lady under cover in Bannack. Nobody saw her leave."

Jim read the letter. "I'm bad luck, Benton. The old stage driver who sought to befriend me was shot down in cold blood. I was the cause of his murder. I was also the cause of the abortive attempt to hang Judge Bryan, who gave me his hand in friendship. I did what I could for him, then sent for you. I hope you can save his life.

"The man who committed these crimes is John Igo. You're next on his killer's list. Go away, Jim Benton, before it's too late, or your blood will be on my hands because you too have been my friend." It was signed "Alison."

Jim Benton put the letter back in the envelope and put it in his pocket. "This letter puts the hangman's noose around John Igo's neck, Barney. I want Judge Bryan to read it when he is well again. Alison should have stayed," he said quietly. "I wanted to talk to her about a lot of things."

There was urgency in his voice when he said, "I've got to make this neck brace." Both men were engrossed in the work of the leather collar when Terry came into the saddle shop with a package under her arm. Both men looked around. Jim Benton blinked his eyes as he stared at the girl, wearing a red-checked gingham dress and black kidskin shoes. A bonnet to match the dress sat saucily on her head. The low yoke showed the tanned neck and modest expanse above the small breasts.

Jim Benton slid from his high stool at the workbench. Wordlessly he took Terry in his arms, holding her close. There was something breathtaking about the clean, wholesome beauty of the girl in gingham that went far beyond description.

Finally Terry pushed Jim away. She held out the package. "The corset," she said, her voice soft. "Get back to work, both of you, while I walk around."

At the workbench, Jim ripped open the package and shook out a black satin corset.

"The best in the store," Terry said. "I've got expensive tastes, Dr. Benton."

"Walk natural."

"I'm practicing," she said, laughing. "It takes years of practice to walk the way that high-chinned Alison McCandless struts around. She used to dance the can-can."

Jim Benton turned his back to her and concentrated on his work. Terry, one hand covering her mouth, stood still. She was staring at the back of Jim's head. "I opened my big mouth," she said, "and put both my big feet into it. I'm sorry if I spoke out of turn, Jim." Her voice sounded stilted.

"It's all right, Terry. Forget it," he said kindly. "And Matt Wagner had nothing to do with the attempt to hang Judge Bryan, Terry."

Barney snorted. "Whatever gave you that idea, lass?"

Jim Benton told her about Alison McCandless' cutting down the Judge and thereby saving his life. "She left town when she saw us riding in. But she left me a note naming the man who tried to hang the Judge. He also murdered Hank Sanford."

"I'm sorry I talked like that about Alison, Jim," Terry said.

Jim held up the stiff collar of saddle leather that was laced down the front. "That ought to do the job," he said, "soon as I put the whalebones in the sheaths and line it with lamb's wool."

VII

Jim Benton was within a couple of miles of the Quarantine Station on Grasshopper Creek when he saw the angry red glow of the fire. Standing high in his stirrups, he lifted the big gelding to a long high trot that chewed up the miles.

He could make out the tongues of flame that licked at the heavy smoke rolling from the tar barrels and drums of creosote. Guns cracked and there was a wild, drunken yip-yipping. A sudden gust of wind swept the smoke away, and Jim caught a glimpse of three or four men on foot running aimlessly, back and forth among the burning buildings.

The pole gate had been swung wide open and tied to a fence post, and the five-strand barb wires cut between every fence post. As Jim Benton reined up, his saddle gun in his hand, he could see that the main house was on fire. Off to the right somebody had set a torch to the big warehouse, and others were throwing kerosene-soaked rags through the bullet-shattered windows of the cowshed laboratory.

As Jim saw the lab shed burst into flame, a cold anger twisted his belly into a bitter knot. He had to fight back the almost uncontrollable urge to spur his horse and to begin shooting at the drunken vandals, who had destroyed years of painstaking research on Texas Tick Fever as related to Rocky Mountain Spotted Fever. The lab had contained countless labeled vials and sealed test tubes, dates and formulas, and carefully compiled records.

Jim Benton's lips were skinned back to show his teeth. His mind was working fast and mentally listing the various chemicals in wholesale bulk within the warehouse. In addition to the drums of creosote and barrels of pine tar and arsenic powder used in the cattle dip, there were large quantities of nitric and sulphuric acids and powdered chemicals, all highly inflammable and explosive. Unaware of the danger of the poisonous fumes in the smoke from the arsenic powder that spewed out from the burning building in a white cloud, the vandals were weaving their way in and out, guns and whisky bottles in their fists, yelling and stumbling around like a bunch of drunken Indians on the warpath.

A tall, huge man, Jim Benton calculated

might be the tough cowhand called Pecos Johnson, lurched out of the white smoke, waving a carbine as he shouted something to his men. Even as he flailed his arms in a warning signal, there came a blinding white glare, followed by a terrific explosion. The heavy roof timbers, partially burned, made flaming rockets that shot a hundred feet in the darkness. The twelve-inch side wall boards split like flaming kindling for a gigantic bonfire.

As the last flat echoes of the cannon-loud explosion rolled across the prairie like thunder and was lost in the night, a pall of silence settled in the thick smoke that blanketed the place. The men who had been yelling and weaving around in drunken glee were no longer there. Their bodies lay torn limb from limb in charred, bloody hunks of flesh and splintered bone. A few horses had been caught with their riders. No living thing had survived the blast and poisonous gases that still layered the ember-strewn ground beneath the black smoke.

Jim Benton had no notion of risking his life by riding closer than he was. He wasted no pity for the men who had sought their own destruction. The only thing he regretted was the obliteration of the long years of research done by Doctor Barnes and those who had risked their lives inside the laboratory to perfect formulas to save livestock and human life.

As Jim Benton sat his horse at the gate, Bill Irvin and his Nester Pool men rode up. They were at camp a half mile down the creek when they heard the explosion.

Jim told Irvin to take his men and head for Bannack before they were shot down by the Spiderweb men. Riding to the Nester Pool camp with Irvin, Jim's eyes had an inward look, as if the vivid picture of the explosion had left its imprint. It would take long years to wipe out that picture from his mind's eye.

With the destruction of the Quarantine Station went his job on Grasshopper Creek. Now he was foot-loose and free to do what he had determined to do when he rode away from Bannack: Find Alison McCandless and block the entry of the Spiderweb trail herds into Montana.

Later, he would make out his report and mail it. But right now, his pen hand was gripping a gun, and he was in a frame of mind to use it.

When Jim Benton rode away from the Nester Pool camp, he traveled an aimless course. Watching the morning star fade and vanish from sight, he was in puzzled thought, wondering if he would find Alison at the Matt Wagner ranch. The man who had carried the package from Doctor Spencer had stopped there. Since the package had held the grim message from Alison McCandless concerning Judge Bryan, there was an odd chance that Alison might have held a rendezvous with the messenger.

Barney had told Jim that the messenger's name was Ribs Parsons from the Hole in the Wall country. Ribs had sided Matt Wagner, Chiz McDougal and Speck's father in their last stand against the Spiderweb gunfighters. Ribs had been badly shot. Cass McCandless had sent him to the State Prison at Deer Lodge, and while there he had been stricken by "galloping consumption." But Judge Bryan had managed a parole for Parsons and Barney had given him a job at his stable. Ribs and Hank Sanford had been cronies, and after Sanford's murder, Barney had sent Ribs out to fetch in the stage coach. It was Ribs who had found the package in the boot under the driver's seat. Barney said it must have been Alison who had sent the ex-convict with the package.

Jim Benton was following a hunch that Alison would need a guide to take her across the rough country to the place where she might find John Igo. He figured she had it planned to kill Igo.

At the Wagner gate, Jim reined up. He was beyond rifle range but within sight of the ranch buildings. At the pole gate with the cowbell attached, he hesitated, knowing he would be a clay pigeon for the rifle in the hands of Matt Wagner.

He had come in search of Alison whom he wanted to see alone. In order to do this, he knew he had to stay alive and in one piece. But once he had convinced her that she was not responsible for Igo's murdering Hank Sanford and the killer's abortive attempt on Judge Bryan's life, and that he, Jim Benton, wanted no part of the Spiderweb outfit, his job was done. Alison was free to go her way and he could go his.

Jim was still undecided what to do when a dry voice came from behind the brush and boulders. "Stand your hand, Benton!"

There was no mistaking that voice. It belonged to Skeeter Owens. It took a few seconds before Jim Benton realized the dangerous spot he was in.

"Throw your guns away!" Skeeter's nasal whine scraped Jim's eardrums.

Angered, Jim said contemptuously, "Ride out into the open, Skeeter. Try taking my guns away."

"I'll do my dickerin' from here. The old man wants you fetched in on the hoof."

"What old man?"

"Cass McCandless. Who the hell else? He got in from Texas last night and is at the headquarters ranch. Sent me to fetch you in and sent Mackin out to find his wife."

"Nothing would please me better than to meet Cass McCandless," Jim Benton said, "but get this straight, Skeeter. I'm keeping my saddle gun and six-shooter. I'll ride to the Spiderweb ranch but not as a prisoner. You can come along or you can go to hell in a hand basket," Jim growled. "Try anything different and you'll have a fight on your hands."

"From where I'm a-settin' you're a dead duck, Benton."

"You scare hell out of a man, Skeeter." Jim slid his six-shooter into plain sight. "I'd as soon shoot my way through your bushwhacker trap as not."

He was telling the truth. He felt as if he had been through some physical ordeal, and the beating had left his senses numb. Right now he was incapable of fear. The scrape of Skeeter's voice was irritating, no

163

more than that. Relaxed in the saddle, he held his thumb on the gun hammer. His eyes, under the slanted hat brim, were cold and indifferent

When Skeeter made no attempt to reply, Jim Benton slacked off his bridle reins and his horse moved ahead at a running walk. "Call off your mangy pack, Skeeter, and let's get on the way," Jim called out.

"I'm alone. I swung past the Quarantine Station and saw you'd had a fire. I took a short cut here, thinking maybe you'd come this way. What happened, Doc?"

"Pecos Johnson, who took Mackin's ramrod job with the Spiderweb, and his drunken gunslingers set fire to the place. The chemicals exploded and blew them all to bits, Pecos included."

"Sonofabitch, I had 'er made to carve on that Pecos gent's kidneys. Him and Curly Mapes were twins."

"He told me his name was Johnson," Jim Benton said. "One of the Johnson Boys, he said."

Skeeter cocked his head sideways. "You mean you never heard tell of the Johnson Boys, Doc?"

"Nope."

"There's a whole damn tribe of the Johnson Boys. Whenever a man hears the owl hoot along the Outlaw Trail, he's one of the Johnson Boys," Skeeter explained.

"That's a new one on me, Skeeter."

"Just like there's a White Elephant Feed and Livery Stable in every town," Skeeter went on, conversationally. "A man on the dodge can get a change of horses and no question asked at any White Elephant stable."

Jim Benton was beginning to enjoy the company of this tough little cowhand. "How come Barney Kelly runs the White Elephant stable at Bannack?" he asked skeptically.

"It was called that long before the Irishman ever came from the Old Country," Skeeter said, then changed the subject. "Pecos came north to gut shoot the man who killed his twin brother. I was fixin' to rip open his belly when Lorne Mackin told him it was a government man called Jim Benton who spilled Curly Mapes' guts on the ground." His wicked little eyes flicked a look at the six-shooter between the pommel of the saddle and Jim's lean belly.

Jim Benton grinned and shoved the gun into its holster. "So that's why he made his tough play in the barroom at the hotel. He had two of his gunslingers with him, but they came out on the losing end." Jim eyed the little knife-man warily. "How come you didn't play your hand out, Skeeter?"

"Mackin made other arrangements. He blames you for Alison McCandless flyin' the coop. Cass tied the can to his tail and put Pecos in as ramrod, so Mackin fixed it for you and Pecos to lock horns, hopin' you'd shoot it out. Mackin's a foxy bastard."

"So far," Jim said, "all he's done is outfox himself."

"The chips ain't all down, Benton." Skeeter's dry laugh had an ominous sound. "When Cass McCandless holds his kangaroo court with Jim Benton and the high-toned Alison on trial, man, oh mister!" His beady eyes glinted wickedly in the sunlight.

"What are we charged with?" Jim Benton's cold tone matched the look in his eyes.

"You want to bust a gut laughin', Doc?"

Jim Benton flushed darkly. Skeeter was no longer amusing. He fought back the fury that churned within him. He shifted his weight to one stirrup so that he could watch the tough little Skeeter.

They rode for a ways in silence. "Which direction did Mackin take to find McCandless' wife, Skeeter?" Jim asked.

"Someone told him she was at Wagner's

place. That's how come I figured on locatin' you there." He cocked his head sideways, knowingly, then added, "Chances are he had you lined in his gun sights. It must have shore itched his trigger finger."

Jim Benton had an uncomfortable feeling. "Why didn't he throw down on me and take me to the Spiderweb?"

"That was my chore. His job is to bring in the woman. Cass told him he'd give him till daybreak tomorrow to find her. If they didn't show up then, he'd send Igo to bring both of you in."

"Is Igo at the Spiderweb?" Jim tried to make it sound matter of fact.

"Nobody but Igo," Skeeter said flat-toned, "ever knows where to locate Igo. Igo's a natural pissant when it comes to bein' in half a dozen places at the same time."

"How do you figure Igo?"

"A genuine double-crossin' sonofabitch."

"I thought that Cass McCandless was with his trail herds." Jim Benton put out another feeler.

"So did everybody, till he rode into the ranch last night, drunk and ornery."

"Cass has those trail herds," Jim said, "due to cross the Montana line in a few days or a week from now. Even with Igo as

Stock Inspector to pass the cattle through the quarantine blockade, it looks like McCandless would be there," he said, watching Skeeter closely, "in case Igo ran into trouble with the government men. Cass has a lot at stake. Too much to just pull out and leave it to his hired hands. Even a wife couldn't be that important."

Skeeter's beady eyes glinted. "You ain't far off in your calculations, Benton. Chances are there'll be a ruckus when they try to pass the Texas cattle across the line. If Igo was to kill a couple of government inspectors, there'd be a big stink. And Cass wants no part of it."

"So he's fixing it ahead of time to be at the ranch, with witnesses to prove his alibi."

"That's the general idea, Benton. Igo's apt to go hawg wild, and Cass wants to keep his hands clean."

"Igo could cross McCandless for us. Use his authority to stop the Spiderweb cattle at the Montana border."

"That ain't likely, Benton. Igo gets five dollars a head for every one of the ten thousand cattle turned loose onto Spiderweb range. It tallies up to about fifty thousand bucks. For that kinda dough, Igo'd kill off a lot of men."

They were close to the Spiderweb head-quarters, when Skeeter said, "You're in for a bad time, Benton."

Jim's hand slid to his gun. "I'm keeping my guns, Skeeter. Is that understood?"

"Make it easy on yourself, Doc," the little man grinned. "Cass said to fetch you in on the hoof. Said nothing about takin' your guns. But if I was you, I wouldn't pull your gun without you got it made to shoot. And you might as well know now as further up the creek, somebody's goin' to kill you before the gunsmoke clears."

"You, Skeeter?"

"Cass pays fightin' wages, Benton. Don't crowd your luck. You can't win for losin' when Cass McCandless deals 'em."

The Spiderweb headquarters' ranch house, a cold, forbidding two-storied granite structure, was located on the summit of a timbered butte, overlooking the vast stretch of open country called the Big Hole.

The house had been built by a British remittance man, who had patterned it after one of the smaller castles in England. Once, it had the look of a Currier & Ives print, with shrubs of all kinds, a bowling green and cricket field. It was a bit of old England on the frontier. Although it was rumored that the Britisher had at one time in his career donned a road-agent's mask, no man was ever more liked than the jovial, fun-loving, hard-riding and hard-drinking Englishman, whose hospitality had become a by-word.

Jim Benton had listened to countless stories about the legendary Britisher who had come West to play cowboy and who had preferred to be called Rawhide, a name given him by Jim Bridger. "Someday, Jim," his father had said, "if you ever get the chance, pay a visit to Rawhide's Castle of the Big Hole."

Now there was little left to remind Jim Benton of the fabulous description his father had given him. Everything had died of neglect. Weeds grew wild. Heavy dust replaced the graveled driveways. Corrals and branding chutes had taken the place of the bowling greens and cricket field.

The granite walls had the appearance of a neglected prison. Stacks of rusted tin cans and old broken boxes were piled at the back of the castle, now known as the rock pile. Where the high-pitched slate roof had been cracked or broken, warped boards and rusted tin patched it. The once proud castle had been stripped of its last vestige of dignity. The forest of lodgepole pines had been destroyed by fire, so that nothing remained but the charred stumps that looked like so many broken and decayed teeth.

The only sound breaking the dismal quiet, as Jim Benton and Skeeter rode up, was the creak of the windmill that needed oiling, and the sound of Cass McCandless, who stood framed in the doorway.

"It took you long enough to get here, Skeeter," Cass growled. "Get down, Benton, and get in here. Take his horse, Skeeter."

Jim Benton swung down from the saddle.

Cass McCandless was a huge man by any standards. He was stripped down to a red flannel undershirt, the legs of his corduroy pants tucked into the high tops of his boots. A pair of silver-mounted spurs were strapped on the boots. A six-inch wide belt, with a double row of brass cartridges, sagged around his heavy paunch. The gun holster was tied down on his thick thigh.

A week's stubble of iron-gray beard marred the line of the heavy jaw. His shock of uncombed hair needed cutting. Steel-gray eyes peered from under shaggy brows. The Winchester gripped in his big, hairy fists, looked like a kid's popgun.

Cass McCandless, yawning as if he had just awakened from a drunken sleep, was surly and dangerous.

Jim Benton left his saddle gun in its scabbard and hitched up his gunbelt. With a slow, deliberate stride, he walked toward the big man blocking the doorway. Jim flicked a glance at the gun pointed at his belly.

"Use that gun, McCandless," Jim said, as his hand gripped the butt of his own six-shooter, "or put it away. I'll live long enough to kill you." His voice was flat.

The windmill creaked. The two men eyed one another.

"How come Skeeter let you keep a gun?" Cass spoke harshly.

"Ask him," Jim Benton replied shortly as he slid his gun out and thumbed the hammer.

Noticing the glassy look in the other man's eyes, Jim knew the big man's reflexes would be slow. Jim could get in the first shot. A split second, and Cass McCandless would be dead. Jim Benton, like a coiled spring, was ready to move in that quick second that meant the difference between life and death.

The gun in McCandless' hands lowered

slowly. "I got things to thrash out between us, Benton." His speech was thick. "Anyhow, I want that Alison bitch I married here when I kill you." He turned and walked down the long narrow hallway, leaving Jim to follow. The slanting rays of sunset filtering through the dusty windows of the gloomy, high-ceilinged tunnel, threw the man's grotesque shadow ahead.

Jim Benton closed the heavy door, and by the time his eyes had become accustomed to the gray gloom, Cass and his gargantuan shadow had vanished. When a shaft of light penetrated the dark end of the long hall, Jim knew that the cowman had opened the door of a lighted room. Making his way cautiously along the hallway, Jim wondered how Alison had stood the confinement of this dark dungeon as long as she had.

The room into which Jim Benton stepped was a replica of a tavern. A semicircular bar with pewter mugs hung on rows of wooden pegs on the wall back of the bar. Where the royal coat of arms had once been displayed, Cass had hung the mounted head of a longhorn Texas bull. Heavy oak tables and armchairs were scattered around the taproom. The hand-adzed hardwood plank floor had long ago lost its lustre. It was dusty and littered with cigar and cigarette butts.

Cass sprawled in a high-backed armchair at a corner table. His carbine leaned against the wall within reach. His six-shooter lay on the table beside a bottle of whisky. An unlit cigar was gripped between his back teeth. One leg was hooked over the arm of the chair.

As Jim Benton entered the room, Cass waved a hand toward the bar. "Shut the door, Benton. Help yourself to what liquor them damned servants left when Mackin run 'em off. Had a dozen colored bastards I fetched up from Texas to cook and keep the place clean and wait on that chippy I'm married to. The place's a gawddamned boar's nest."

Cass swung both feet up on the table, the spur rowels hooked into the scarred top. He pulled a match across the chair bottom and set fire to the end of his cigar.

"Fetch your drink, Benton, and draw up a chair," he said. "By hell, you've given me a lot of trouble, right from the start when you knifed me in the back at the Stock-growers' meeting." His bloodshot eyes glared at Jim. "I got four big herds of cattle on the trail from Texas. One is nothing but longhorns, a mixed bunch, all horns and bushy tails. The whole two thousand ain't worth two bits, but I was born and raised with longhorned cattle. They got a sentimental value and I can afford to raise them just for the hell of it."

Sitting down, Jim smiled inwardly. Without half trying he had found the weak spot in this big, ruthless Texan.

As Cass took a swallow of whisky, a shudder shook his big frame. "I been gone a month. Left Mackin to run the outfit, and what the hell happens?" He banged the glass tumbler on the arm of the chair with such force that it shattered in his fist. He shook the broken glass to the floor, then looked at the small cut places in his calloused palm. Raising his hand close to his eyes, he picked out shards of glass and wiped the blood off on his undershirt.

"I'll tell you what I found, Benton," Cass continued. "The Spiderweb outfit shot to hell and gone. My ramrod on a big drunk. Sundown, the town I built from scratch, shot up." He swung his spurred boots to the floor and his bloodshot eyes stared at Jim Benton and held for a long moment. "Until you showed up, things were running smooth. You're a gawddamned trouble maker, Benton."

Jim Benton smiled grimly, his eyes wary.

"Spit it out," he said.

"All right. My wife's quit me." A glitter crept into the cowman's eyes. "On account of you, Benton," he added.

"A lie," Jim said quietly. "A damned, malicious lie."

"When Mackin gets here with that bitch wife of mine," Cass said, "we'll go into it then. I got ways of culling the lies from the truth, Benton." He took a long pull from the bottle, shuddered and coughed. He eyed the label. "Bottled in bond, ten years old," he read. He coughed again. "Damned stuff tastes like rotgut."

The man's eyes were congested. He was breathing hard; sucking air and blowing. The cigar crumpled in his clenched fist. One hand tore at the buttons on his undershirt, popping them, ripping the shirt apart to show the hair-matted barrel chest. Beads of sweat came from the coarse pores of his skin, as he gasped for breath like a wind-broken old stallion.

Jim eyed him critically. McCandless seemed on the verge of apoplexy.

Cass yanked a handkerchief from his hip pocket and mopped his face. "Mackin and Alison had it made to kill me off." Cass was back on the subject that was bothering him, showing his jealous hate. "All Mackin had to do was shoot me in the back and the pair of them could travel high, wide and handsome, with the Spiderweb in his pocket. He stood better than an even chance to swing it, till you showed up and spoiled the batter. The bitch spit in his face when you landed in Sundown."

"Who brought you up to date on all this, McCandless?" Jim Benton sat tense in his chair. The big cowman was getting close to the truth.

"Mackin had orders to ride herd on my wife. Skeeter had orders to keep an eye on Mackin. Igo had orders to stay in the background and keep his eyes open and his ears to the ground." Cass showed his teeth in a wicked grin.

Jim Benton rolled a quick cigarette. His eyes looked bleak through the tobacco smoke. "Who," he asked coldly, "did you hire to watch Igo?"

"Nobody. Who the hell could keep an eye on that spook bastard? You look for Igo and he's long gone."

"You sent a big, tough gent called Pecos Mapes, with gravel for brains, to take over Igo's job. You know where Pecos Mapes is right now, big mister?"

"Where he should be. Ramrodding the roundup."

Jim Benton shook his head. "Pecos Mapes is in hell, along with several of his tough hands. He set fire to the Quarantine Station. The chemicals stored there blew them to hell and gone."

"You wouldn't lie to a man, Benton?"

Jim Benton fixed a cold look at the big man. "It's about time you balanced your books. You're in the red, McCandless, and the red ink is human blood." Jim dropped his cigarette butt into a cuspidor.

Cass took a long pull at the bottle, coughed and spat on the floor. "I got a gut ache. Don't give me no sermons, Benton. To hell with it. Let the dead bury the dead." He wiped his hands on his undershirt. "Hired hands like Pecos and the others come a dime a dozen down in the Panhandle."

"This isn't the Panhandle. Sit back and I'll check them off, McCandless. Mackin and Skeeter killed Curly Mapes, then hung Felix Carruthers, the postmaster. Your hired killer Igo, whom you sprung out of prison, killed an unarmed stage driver named Hank Sanford. Not satisfied with Sanford's murder, he put a noose around the neck of Judge Bryan and left him for dead. The laws of Montana will hold you responsible for the actions of these men who are all in your employ."

"They'll play hell proving anything. Igo's on his own. He has a law badge."

"Your name is signed to his parole papers. That holds you responsible. You got him that Stock Inspector's badge."

"I signed no papers that can incriminate me. I got a lawyer who attends to that. Hell, there's no way to prove I got Igo out of jail. Even the money used to grease a few palms can't be traced to me."

Jim decided there wasn't any use in trying to argue with a man like Cass McCandless.

Cass lifted the bottle. "Listen to me, you two-bit government thing," he went on. "I'm fetching my four trail herds across your quarantine line. Them with tick fever will die off, but the bulk of the ten thousand will winter on Spiderweb range. Any dipping to be done will be done right here. To hell with you. You'll give me no more trouble of any kind, Benton." He took another drink, shuddered and coughed.

Jim Benton watched the sweat bead the man's whiskered face and saw that the red undershirt was sodden.

Cass was at it again, his voice harsh. "Where I come from a man can kill any picayune trifling sonofabitch who monkeys around with his wife. It's the unwritten law of Texas. They don't even arrest the husband of a faithless wife. He never comes to trial." He leaned forward, banging his big fist on the table. His face was blotched as he choked with an anger getting beyond control. A trembling racked him until his teeth chattered and he leaned back in the big chair.

"— damn malaria — picked it up in Mexico when I was a kid — comes back on a man — sudden —" The words came haltingly from behind clenched teeth as he watched Jim Benton with fever-glazed eyes. "Be all right — directly the liquor takes hold —"

Tense-muscled, Jim Benton sat on the edge of the chair. He said quietly, "You woke up this morning with a backache. Your vision was blurred, joints stiff. You got a chill and then you burned up with fever. How about it, McCandless?"

"Hell, yes — damned malaria — hits a man — be all right —"

"Somewhere along the trail a cattle tick fastened to your skin. Maybe you remember, McCandless?"

"Hell, yes — on my belly. I watched him fill up with blood — then I punctured the purple sac with the point of my knife.

180

Pecos — liked to bust a gut — laughing."

"The tick head is still buried under your skin," Jim Benton said flatly. "You're not fighting a short bout with malaria, McCandless. It's Rocky Mountain Spotted Fever you've got, caused by the bite of a cattle tick. All the things you've complained about are Spotted Fever symptoms."

Jim got slowly to his feet. "Tonight or tomorrow or maybe the following day the chills and fever will give way to delirium. You'll be a raving maniac from then till you die a violent death in about ten days. The cattle King of the Panhandle should get a big belly laugh out of it. Pecos Mapes should come back from hell to join you."

Jim Benton, not proud of his little speech, had to force every brutal word from his mouth. "Dr. Spencer sent me a package of tick serum. If I had one little vial of it with me, I might save your life, but it was destroyed when Pecos Mapes and your Spiderweb vandals blew up the Quarantine Station lab."

Jim turned his back and stood staring out the window into the gathering night. He had given Cass McCandless his death verdict in the only manner the big cattleman could understand. There was nothing to do now except watch the man die.

The only sound in the room was the labored breathing of Cass McCandless. Then suddenly his voice crashed between the rock walls. "You're lying, Benton. No man on earth can throw that kind of a scare into me." The .45 exploded in his big fist. The bullet whined past Jim's head, missing it by scant inches.

The shock of it spun Jim around and, grabbing the untouched bottle of bourbon from the table, he brought it down with a short chopping blow on the thick-matted head. The bottle smashed, spilling whisky and splintered glass. The gun slid from McCandless' hand and his head lobbed forward.

Jim looked down at the motionless cowman. He was unaware that Skeeter Owens had come into the stone-walled room until he heard the nasal voice behind him and felt the needling pain of a knife point in his back. The dry chuckle had the sound of a rattler before it struck.

"I'm still on the Spiderweb payroll, Benton. Make a move and I'll rip your kidneys out."

Jim Benton froze in his tracks. His head was turned enough to see the evil grin on the wizened face. A murderous look showed in the beady eyes.

"Drop that knife!" That was Alison's voice. It came from outside the door that Skeeter had left open.

Jim saw the little knife man's head turn quickly, and in that split second he spun around. His left hook caught the point of Skeeter's jaw, breaking the jawbone. Skeeter was lifted off his feet with the weight of the blow. Jim Benton grabbed him as he fell backwards and flung him against the stone wall, where he fell motionless to the floor.

The acrid fumes of burnt gunpowder from McCandless' gun still hung in the air when Alison came into the room, a .38 pistol gripped in her hand. She smiled grimly. Flicking a glance at Skeeter, she stood beside the chair looking down at the slumped man she had married. She looked up at Jim Benton, and said, "Dead?"

Jim bent over McCandless, his fingers on the pulse in the thick wrist. "He's alive," he said, "but he'll be dead in ten days. Spotted Fever. He claimed it was malaria."

"There's no cure?" Alison's eyes were on a level with his.

"The only cure," Jim Benton replied, "was in that package of serum Dr. Spencer sent. It was destroyed when the Spiderweb outfit set fire to the Station. If I had just one small vial of that vaccine, there might be a chance. . . ." His words trailed off. Something he had forgotten flashed through his brain.

Jim crossed the floor to Skeeter. He turned him over on his back, shaking him. "Come alive, Skeeter. Where did you put my saddlebags?" Then he noticed the face with the jawbone caved in. The man looked dead enough to bury. "I guess my saddlebags are at the stable," Jim said. "Would you mind getting them —"

Alison was nowhere in the room as he turned around. Her absence sent a chill into his guts. He remembered that McCandless had sent Lorne Mackin to bring in his wife. There had been neither time nor opportunity to ask Alison if she had come alone, or where Mackin was. In the lamplit room, he was a plain target for any bushwhacker outside. Aware of this danger, his hand slid to his gun.

A dull crash behind him turned him quickly around. Then he saw what had caused the noise. The high-backed chair that held McCandless' huge bulk had over-turned. Cass was trying to get to his hands and knees, shaking his head sluggishly from side to side, mouthing incoherently. The whole thing was like an actual nightmare.

The cowman was crawling slowly on all fours, for all the world like a wounded grizzly, shaking his lobbing head, filling the room with jumbled blasphemy. Jim Benton steadied Cass' rolling weight while he crossed the hall and entered a bedroom. Jim lit the lamp and somehow managed to roll the big man up onto the high four-poster bed and over on his back.

Alison came in with the saddlebags. Jim found the vial of serum and explained that it was the serum mixed from ground-up cattle ticks. "Cass is in the first stages of the disease. With this injection I should know in twelve hours if the fever is checked," he told her. Jim sawed the sealed end of the vial with a tiny file he took from the hypodermic case, sterilized the needle and glass syringe with grain alcohol and swabbed the hairy arm. For a long moment he studied the big cowman who lay sweating and helpless, and then he injected the tick serum. Together Jim and Alison cut away the man's clothes and sponged him off, then covered him with a clean sheet and blanket.

Jim Benton was putting the hypodermic case back into his saddlebags, when he asked casually, "Did Lorne Mackin bring you here, Alison?"

"Lorne Mackin is dead," she said. "Ribs Parsons shot him and tied him to the saddle for me to turn over to Cass McCandless." Her thin smile sent a shiver through him.

"Skeeter was ready to kill me," Jim said. "I'm in your debt for saving my life, Alison. Anything I can do for you to repay that debt, I'll do."

"You'd be surprised if I took you up on that. Called your bluff," she said. "And let that be a lesson to you, Benton."

Alison walked over to the door and closed it, locking it from the inside. She stood with her back to the door, a peculiar expression on her face.

"Let's get this thing straight, Benton. You're making a desperate effort to save Cass' life, knowing that if he gets well, he will kill you and destroy me . . ."

"I have no choice in the matter," Jim Benton answered. "Your husband is in the primary stages of a fatal disease that will kill him within ten days, unless that vaccine reacts as it should. If it does, and Cass McCandless lives, that's all that matters." Excitement crept into his voice when he added, "Can't you see, Alison, I'll be the first man to cure a human being with Dr.

Spenny's tick juice vaccine! Me, a common vet!"

For the first time the harsh lines around her mouth erased the flinty look in her green eyes. When she smiled, the transformation was complete. She took a tentative step toward him, then stopped. "You're the doctor," she said, putting meaning into the title.

Jim Benton and Alison stood without speaking for a while, then with bitterness darkening her eyes, she said, "I'm bad luck, Benton. Old Hank Sanford saw its long black shadow when he shoved me down under the seat a moment before Igo blasted him. Hank fell on top of me. I was knocked out. When I came to, I had to crawl out from under his dead body. I found my horse and rode to Bannack." A long sigh escaped between her lips and she began to pace the floor. "I stabled my horse and hid out until the town was asleep. I crawled out of the hay loft and went up to Judge Bryan's rooms. When he didn't answer my knock, I pushed open the door that was slightly ajar. You know the rest. And for some reason I know I am the cause of what happened to him." She would have turned away, but Jim took her by both shoulders.

"You weren't to blame for the murder of Hank Sanford or for the attempt on Judge Bryan's life." He shook her until she looked up at him. "You must believe that, Alison." He showed her the scrap of paper with the numbers 3-7-77, explaining the meaning of the warning pinned to Hank's shirt. He went on to tell her about John Igo's near-hanging in the Vigilante days.

"Stay here, Alison," Jim said. "I've got to check up on Skeeter."

When Jim Benton went into the tap-room, Skeeter was gone. Stepping outside, Jim hardly raised his voice. "You're out there somewhere, Skeeter," he said. "I need you. Cass is a hell of a sick man, down with Rocky Mountain Spotted Fever. In ten days he'll be dead unless you help. You're still on the Spiderweb payroll, Skeeter. Earn your wages." Jim stopped talking long enough to roll a cigarette and light it; then he went on.

"Get an empty bottle, Skeeter. What I need right now is about a dozen cattle ticks. Don't get any that are sucking blood. Pick the ones you find crawling around on the hide. I'm fighting to save the life of McCandless, Skeeter. I know what I'm doing. I'll need that bottle of live ticks in

188

an hour from now. Earn your fighting wages, man."

There was a long wait. Jim Benton stubbed out his cigarette and went inside, leaving the door open. By the time he was halfway down the hall Skeeter showed in the doorway. He had a dirty black handkerchief tied under his broken jaw, the corners knotted on top of his head. His beady eyes were bloodshot and wicked.

"I'll be back, directly, Doc," His words were uneven and blurred. "I butchered a beef this mornin'. The hide is crawlin' with ticks. I'll get me a bottle from the taproom." Skeeter sidled down the hall into the taproom.

Alison's shadowy form filled the bedroom door. She had Jim's gun in her hand. He had removed it and the cartridge belt when he had helped McCandless into bed.

"There's supposed to be a special guardian angel that protects drunks and children," she said, her face chalky. "You're not drunk and you're no longer a kid. Buckle this on, Benton. Keep it on." Her voice was tight.

When Skeeter Owens came into the room with the bottle of cattle ticks, Jim Benton was beside the bed taking the sick man's pulse. Alison was on the opposite side of the bed.

Cass McCandless' eyes were closed under heavy lids. His skin had a dry, gray pallor, the color and texture of dry putty. Jim removed the thermometer from the parched lips, frowning a little at the reading. He answered the question in Skeeter's beady eyes.

"Still on the losing end. Running a high temperature. Pulse ragged."

"He looks dead," Skeeter muttered.

Jim Benton pulled back the covers and showed Skeeter the swollen, purplish spot where the tick had fastened itself. "Unless the vaccine I'm using wins out, Cass McCandless will be dead in a few days." He pulled the covers up.

Jim took the bottle of ticks and put them on a marble top washstand. The layers of moving ticks were inches thick at the base.

"I was listenin' outside," Skeeter volunteered the information, "while you gave the boss his verdict. You shore didn't hold nothin' back, Benton."

"All right, feller. So I told it to him scary." Jim's eyes narrowed. "You're good at eavesdropping. What else did you hear?"

"All of it," Skeeter said. He cut Alison a look, and said, "You did a good job on Lorne Mackin, lady."

Alison smiled thinly. "You figure on playing out his dead hand, little weasel?"

"Depends," Skeeter said, holding his jaw cupped in his hand. "If Cass dies, I ain't workin' no more for the Spiderweb."

"That's right, Skeeter," Alison told him. "If Cass dies, I'm sole owner of the outfit. I'll pay you off providing you're still alive to collect your fighting pay."

"If you're through with me here, Benton," Skeeter said, "I got a job to tend to."

"Sit down, Skeeter," Jim Benton said. "After I give Cass a heart stimulant, I'll set your broken jaw before the swelling gets any worse."

Skeeter backed into the hall, Jim Benton following.

"You lay a hand on me, it'll be your hard luck, Doc," Skeeter warned as he picked up the Winchester he had left leaning against the wall. Backing down the hall to the main door, he made a sinister-looking figure with the saddle gun in the crook of his arm. "One thing, Doc," he said. "So long as you keep Cass McCandless alive, you're safe."

"And if he dies?" Jim Benton asked.

"Then me'n' you pick up where we left off." Skeeter pulled the outside door closed.

Jim Benton returned to the bedroom where he prepared the medicine and gave it to the cowman. Sitting on the edge of the bed, he kept his face expressionless while he felt the pulse of the sick man. After a while the set lips relaxed and he turned toward Alison.

"That was a close shave, Alison. I wasted a lot of precious time on Skeeter. No pulse at all. I thought Cass was a goner." He looked at his watch. "Five minutes till midnight," he said aloud. Walking over to the washstand, he held the bottle of ticks up to the light for a few moments, then put it down.

From the saddlebags he took a small-sized mortar and pestle which he cleansed with alcohol and let them dry. Then he ground the ticks into a thick paste. Into it he measured carbolic acid from an eye-dropper until the paste became liquid. Drawing some of his own blood from his arm, he mixed it slowly with the tick juice. Then he filled the syringe.

"You watched me treat the paste with carbolic acid, Alison," he said. "That was a precaution I took, just in case some of those ticks had consumed even a small drop of the animal's blood. Research discovered that carbolic acid kills the deadly germs in ticks that might have sucked some blood." Jim Benton gave the cowman another injection. "God knows I've taken enough risks as it is," he added.

"Quit handicapping yourself with worry." Alison laid a hand on his arm. "He's not worth it."

"You don't understand, Alison. I undertook the job of saving the life of a human being, regardless of who the man is."

Alison looked at him as a mother might look at a headstrong child. "Tend to your patient, Doctor," she said. "I'll clean up this mess."

Jim bent over the sick man. He put a hand to Cass' forehead, placed the thermometer in his mouth and checked the pulse. "It's waiting that tries a man's nerves," he said.

It was two-thirty in the morning when Jim Benton marked down with a laborious hand what he told himself might be the last recording. Cass McCandless might not even last the extent of the usual ten days' time. No man could survive the high fever and live for any length of time.

The strain of it showed in Jim Benton's unshaven face. Defeat dulled his eyes and his face was gaunt and gray. Reaching for the loaded syringe with an unsteady hand, he gave the cowman another injection for the heart. The pulse beat was feeble and the fever at its highest. Two minutes by the second hand on Jim's watch and the pulse beat became stronger and steady. The temperature dropped one degree.

Ten minutes later he told Alison to close all the windows and to get more blankets. McCandless was sweating from every pore in his big body.

Jim Benton had tossed the coin: Death on the black side, Life on the other.

Like a man shucking off a heavy overcoat, Jim Benton shook off the utter exhaustion. The color returned to his face. Sparks glinted in his eyes. He downed the drink of whisky Alison shoved into his hand.

Jim Benton had won his odds on the battle against death.

VIII

Cass McCandless' eyes blinked open. For a while they stared dully into space, seeing nothing. Slowly, as memory stirred inside the brain that had gone vacant during the long black hours, the blank stare left the sick eyes. They swiveled in dark sockets and came to rest on Alison's face. She met the turmoil of the hate-filled eyes without flinching. Then Cass' stare turned to Jim Benton.

Jim, understanding the man's frustration and bitterness, saw the lust to kill in the sick man's eyes. He knew that McCandless was unaware of the close brush with death but starkly aware of being helpless for the first time in his ruthless career.

"All right if I open a window?" Alison spoke quietly.

"The room could stand some fresh air," Jim Benton said.

The sharp crack of a 30-30 Winchester sounded as Alison parted the drapes and opened a window. She jerked her head aside in time to miss the hornet-whine of a bullet that flattened against the stone wall on the far side of the room.

A man's hate-crazed laugh came through the gun echoes. "Scared the peewaddin' outa that painted chippy!" The voice belonged to Matt Wagner. "Come out from behind your wife's skirts, McCandless. Have a gun in your hand, you Texican son of a bitch!"

The big man in the bed was trying desperately to sit up. He cursed in dry sobs as he fell back weakly.

Jim Benton turned off the light. He moved to the window and crouched beside Alison. Matt Wagner began to shoot again, the bullet showering them with shards of shattered window glass. Jim waited until Matt had emptied his carbine.

Standing up, he called to Matt. "Hold your fire, Wagner. Jim Benton talking. McCandless is sick, too weak to get out of bed."

Then old Chiz McDougal's creaky voice sounded outside in the early dawn. "It's me 'n' you, Matt. I'm givin' you a chance for your taw!"

Two guns exploded within split seconds. Matt Wagner's scream was a banshee wail, cut off in death. Through the shots and scream cut the razor-sharp voice of

Skeeter, pounding on the barred bedroom door. "Lemme in," his voice was thin. "I'm shot to hell!"

"Don't, Jim," Alison whispered in the dark room. "He'll knife you."

"Get behind the door and have your gun ready, if he's lying," Jim told her. Jim Benton slid the bolt and pulled open the door cautiously. Skeeter was on all fours, dragging a wounded leg. He had the knife in his hand. It was wet with fresh blood.

Jim Benton let him crawl inside and to the bed. "You alive, Cass?" Skeeter asked.

"Too tough to die, Skeeter. Who shot you?" Cass asked.

"Ribs Parsons shot me in the leg before I cut his throat. Gimme a tussle when I jumped his back."

"Loan me your gun," Cass whispered weakly.

Jim Benton crossed to the bed in a couple of long-legged strides. He twisted the gun from Skeeter's hand, then grabbed the wrist that held the knife, his blunt thumb digging into the nerve. The knife dropped to the floor. Jim kicked it under the bed and pushed Skeeter Owens into a chair.

"I'll look you over, Skeeter," he told him, "when I get around to it. Meanwhile, sit straddle of that chair and don't move."

From outside Old Chiz McDougal was calling Jim Benton's name. Jim moved to the window and called out, "What's on your mind, Chiz?"

"Did Matt hit you, Doc?"

"Just a close miss. No harm done. Who's out there with you, Chiz?"

"Matt Wagner. He's dead." Chiz spoke with vitriolic tongue. "Ribs Parsons has his throat cut. They had it made to kill Cass McCandless. He got a gun in your back, Doc?"

"Nobody has a gun in my back, Chiz. Cass is sick as a poisoned pup. In bed, too weak to wipe his own nose."

"It's about time," Chiz said, bitter sarcasm honed into the words, "that you quit playin' like a damnfool hero. Cass ain't goin to whittle out no rawhide medal to pin on your dead carcass."

"I'm pulling the curtains, Chiz," Jim Benton said, "and lighting the lamp. Nobody's stopping you if you want to come in."

"How about Skeeter?" asked Chiz.

"Skeeter's on ice."

"I'm comin' in, Doc."

Jim Benton pulled the drapes and Alison lit the lamp. Jim slid the lock on the door and Old Chiz stepped into the room, his gun in his hand, taking in what there was to see in a few seconds. Putting his gun back into its holster, he limped over to the bed and stared down at the sick man's hate-filled eyes.

"That's a hell of a way for a man to die," he said. "In bed, like a gentle Annie." Chiz turned away to look at Skeeter, giving him a crooked grin.

"You gimpy-legged, two-bit nester," Cass croaked.

Old Chiz chuckled. "Dyin', hell!" he said. "There's nothin' wrong with the cattle king of the Panhandle that a jug of likker won't cure."

Old Chiz limped over to Skeeter straddling the chair. "You got lump jaw?" Chiz was having himself a time.

Before Skeeter could reply, Jim Benton put a bottle of liquor into his hand. "Pain killer," he said. "You'll need it."

He waited while Skeeter drank a couple of big gulps, then told him to get a tight grip on the chair. He felt along both sides of the swollen jaw, jutting out at an angle. "No fracture. Just a dislocation." Jim Benton gave a quick sideways jerk with tightened hands, and the dislocated jaw slipped back into place. Skeeter let out a howl of pain and then passed out.

While Skeeter was out like Nellie's eye, Jim Benton cut away the pants leg and using raw whisky to sterilize the open gunshot wound in the man's leg, he wrapped a tight bandage around it. Skeeter groaned and blinked open his eyes.

Jim saw Cass McCandless watching him. "You did a good job on Skeeter," Cass said grudgingly.

"How about the job Jim Benton did on you?" Alison put in sharply.

"I wouldn't know about that. Or what went on while I was passed out." The bitter hate was back.

McCandless watched Jim Benton pick up his things on the washstand and put them neatly into the saddlebags. Jim picked up the bottle of crawling ticks and held it up for the cowman to see. "Cattle ticks," he said. "I ground up some of them into serum and shot it into your veins. Apparently that's what cured you, for you certainly were in the first stages of Rocky Mountain Spotted Fever."

"To be beholdin' to the dirty son of a bitch who stole my wife while I was away is unshirted hell," Cass gritted between clenched teeth. "Igo gave me the will Alison made, leaving her share of the

Spiderweb to you, Benton. He took it from Judge Bryan's office."

"I don't want any part of the Spiderweb, McCandless," said Jim Benton. "And there's never been anything wrong between your wife and myself."

"When a man's wife," Cass said bitterly, "makes out her will, giving all she owns to her lover, it's all the proof a man needs, Benton."

Alison turned from the window to face her husband. Her lips curled back. "I offered Jim Benton everything I owned, along with my body," she said. "He turned me down cold. Benton wouldn't touch me or the Spiderweb with a ten-foot pole."

Cass McCandless lay back, his eyes dulled by the contempt and loathing in the woman's voice. He had nothing more to say.

Jim crossed the room to get his hat and coat hanging from the elk antlers. As he reached for his coat, he stepped on something on the floor and bent over to pick it up. It was a leather vest pocket tally book that must have slipped out of McCandless' pocket.

His back to the cattleman, Jim fanned the pages with his thumb. Midway through, his attention fixed on the carefully outlined map, showing the Beaver-head Mountain range. Below each arrow that pierced the mountain range were the printed names: BANNACK PASS, LEMHI PASS, SPIDERWEB PASS, and LOST TRAIL PASS.

On the side of the Beaverhead Mountains was printed IDAHO; on the other MONTANA. On the Montana side a red ink outline marked the Spiderweb Range. Inside was a small circle marked Head-quarters Ranch, just below the SPIDERWEB PASS.

Jim studied it for a brief moment, then leafed over to the next page. His brows pulled together in a slight frown. It took no longer than a half minute for him to digest the facts. The four trail herds were coming from the Idaho side of the mountains to be spilled onto the Spiderweb range.

Only one trail herd was given a name: Longhorn herd, due to come through Spiderweb Pass on July 4th. The others were designated by numbers: No. 1 herd due Lost Trail Pass, July 6th; No. 2 through Lemhi Pass, July 8th, and No. 3 through Bannack Pass, July 10th.

Underneath was a notation: "Igo will be on hand to inspect and pass the trail herds. After all four herds have been delivered onto Spiderweb range, Igo will collect his fee of five dollars per head. There should be ten thousand head of Texas cattle."

Jim Benton had kept his back turned while he absorbed this vital information. He slid the tally book into his coat pocket as he took it from the antlers. He doubted that anyone had observed what he was doing. He shrugged into his coat and reached for his hat. Picking up his saddlebags, he slung them over one shoulder and walked to the bed.

"You're on your own from here on, McCandless," Jim told him.

"How much do I owe you, Benton?" McCandless' tight-lipped mouth twisted sardonically.

"Not a damned thing, mister." Jim Benton turned and crossed the room to speak to Alison. "There's nothing to keep you here now. I'll ride with you as far as Bannack."

"Get out," Cass said coldly. "And to hell with both of you. Take the old nester son of a bitch with you," he croaked. "Skeeter's stayin'."

As the two men and the girl left the room, Alison said to Skeeter as she passed him, "Keep the king alive, little man. Once he's gone, you're a goner, too."

At the barn, Jim said grimly, "Saddle up and let's get out of gun range. We'll take the lower trail, keeping the corrals between us and the main house, in case either of them in there take a notion for a little target practice."

When they were safely out of gun range, they pulled down to a long high trot. A mile or so farther on, they halted and dismounted.

Squatted on boot heels, Jim Benton showed them the tally book. "It's been twenty years or longer," he said, "since the last cattle drive came up the trail from Texas to Montana. They've been shipped by train for years."

"Likely shipped by train to Idaho," Old Chiz commented. "Unloaded and driven across country and turned loose on free range the other side of the Beaverhead Mountains, with enough Spiderweb cowhands to keep the cattle from straying."

"Why should they unload the cattle in Idaho?" asked Alison.

"There are only two railway lines into Montana," Jim explained. "Right now, at each railroad town on the Montana border, there are government and state stock inspectors waiting to stop the cattle trains bringing in the Spiderweb cattle from Texas. They're due for a long wait."

"I get it," said Alison. "While the inspectors wait for the cattle trains, the four herds are being driven through the gaps in the mountains."

"That's right," Jim said. He read aloud the four passes through which the cattle would be driven and closed the tally book.

"I want you to ride to Bannack, Alison," Jim said. "Give this tally book to the Town Marshal. Tell Barney Kelly I want him to get hold of Bill Irvin, the man who ramrods the Nester Pool. Have him get every nester deputized and tell Irvin to put about ten men at each of the passes except the Spiderweb pass in time to make a Winchester cut on the Spiderweb cattle as they come through." Jim handed her the book.

"Go along with Alison, Chiz. See that she gets to Bannack, unharmed," Jim told him.

"Whichaway for you, Doc?"

"Spiderweb Pass. My guess is that John Igo will be there. It's my job to put Igo on ice."

"Igo is a professional killer, Doc," Old Chiz said waspishly. "Made a tough rep shootin' fellers like you in the back. I'm goin' along."

"That's right, Chiz," Alison said emphatically. "Benton's not cold-blooded enough to kill Igo on sight. And he's too good a man to get murdered. Ride close herd on him, Chiz."

Alison mounted and rode off at a long trot without a backward look.

Old Chiz's faded blue eyes watched horse and rider until they were lost in the dust.

"It takes a thoroughbred to go the distance," he said, lifting a bottle of whisky in a salute. There was no way of knowing whether the old cowpuncher meant the black filly or the woman in the saddle. He shoved the bottle into Jim's hands. "I'll keep Skeeter from knifin' you in the back, Doc, if you want to pick it up where you left off with McCandless."

"You mean kill him?"

"You let that big Texican live and he'll kill you. Deal his wife hell on earth. You'll never have a better chance."

"McCandless is a sick man, Chiz," Jim said. "About twelve hours ago he showed positive symptoms of the first stages of Rocky Mountain Spotted Fever. It took a hell of a strong constitution to survive. If he lives ten days without a recurrence, then I can pat myself on the back. And if I had my way and the time, I'd stay with him for the next ten days."

Old Chiz groaned dismally. "I hope to hell Igo ain't down with a runny nose or a gut ache."

After that they rode in silence, each man busy with his own thoughts. Finally, when the grizzled old cowhand spoke, his softened voice blended into the quiet.

"It musta been in the cards," he said, "for me to kill Matt."

It brought Jim Benton back sharply from his dark musings. He blurted out a belated gratitude. "It slipped my mind. Matt would have killed me. To save me you killed your lifelong friend."

"I had it made to kill Matt long before you came into the deal, Doc. Years ago. But I kept putting it off, hopin' somebody would take the job off my hands. All the time I knew it was up to me to kill the son of a bitch. It's been a long time since there was any friendship wasted between me'n' Matt Wagner. Fact is, I've hated his guts for so long it got to be a habit." He shook his head sideways and gave Jim Benton a wry grin. "He come from good honest folks, good breeding stock. But Matt Wagner was as low down as they come. It don't figure, Doc."

"There's always a throwback, Chiz. Or

maybe there was something in Matt's early boyhood that brought out the mean streak. Would that be before your time, Chiz?"

"Hell, no. I've knowed Matt since he was stirrup high." He dismissed it with an impatient gesture. "Could be you hit the nail on the head. Guess I've knowed it all along."

"What was the trouble at the start, Chiz?"

"Religion," Chiz said emphatically. "Too damned much religion. Old man Wagner was a circuit rider preacher. Rode a white mule, preachin' religion to cowboy sinners. When I got mixed up in the Wire Cutters' War in Texas, old man Wagner saved my life. I was shot to hell, sittin' on a stolen horse with a rope around my neck and throwed over the limb of an oak tree, when old man Wagner rode out of the brush on his white mule. He cut me down and scared off the line riders. Took me to his little ranch and gave me a home."

Old Chiz quit talking, his eyes as bleak as the overcast sky. Jim Benton was beginning to understand things that had been puzzling him. He wanted the grizzled cowhand to continue, but the look in his eyes forbade questioning.

"When Wagner and his wife both died of

malaria in the same week, they made me promise to look after their hell-raisin' son. I was a few years older than Matt, and a range orphan, and I helped old man Wagner build up the ranch. I was willed a half interest. After their funeral Matt got into trouble knifin' another kid over a little Mexican puta. I kept the Ranger who'd come to arrest him busy while Matt saddled up and rode out. That night I met him and we crossed the Texas border into the Indian Nation before sunrise. That was only the start. From then on Matt held the promise I'd made his folks over my head like a double-bitted axe."

Chiz went back across the years, uncovering the tracks he had buried for young Matt Wagner. He had taken the rap for Matt on a cattle-stealing charge and had been sent to prison for ten years. "I'd been there yet only Judge Bryan got me pardoned. He got suspicious when Matt filed a claim to get my share of the Wagner outfit I'd built up while he was off with Ribs Parsons stealin' horses and rustlin' cattle."

"Did Ribs Parsons go to prison with you?" Jim Benton asked.

"Ribs went over the road for a life stretch, but not for the same reason. He shot one of the Spiderweb night riders and got railroaded to the pen by Lorne Mackin."

Again the old cowpuncher lapsed into silence. This time it seemed to be a different kind of wordless brooding, as if he were trying to decide whether or not to get it out of his system.

"Damn it to hell, Doc," he finally blurted out. "A man ain't blind, and I'd have to be deaf, dumb and blind as a bat not to know how it is between you and McCandless' wife."

Jim felt his face redden. But he met the other man's probing question without flinching. "You were there, Chiz," Jim said, "when I told McCandless there was nothing wrong between Alison and me."

"You looked him in the eye, Doc, and lied like a man. I don't want to know a damn thing about it. But she's got her mind made up to marry you once Cass is outa the way. Are you fixin' to marry Cass McCandless' widow?" Chiz asked bluntly.

"No." Jim Benton's voice had a tone of finality. "Once this thing is over and if I'm all in one piece, I'm going to marry Terry, if she'll have me. You're wrong about Alison McCandless wanting to marry me,

Chiz. I wouldn't lie about a thing like that."

"Guess I had it figured wrong."

"Any man can be wrong, Chiz," Jim Benton said.

"It's a load off my mind, Doc," Chiz said quietly. "If you was to hurt Terry, I'd have to kill you. And I'd hate to have to kill a young feller I've taken a likin' to."

"I'd never lift a hand to stop you, Chiz."

"I saw Terry's mother go through hell married to Matt."

"Terry told me about it," Jim said.

"A man in the pen has plenty of time to think things out," Chiz said. "When I got out, I had it made to get back the outfit Matt stole from me and give him the damnedest workin' over a man ever lived through. But Ribs Parsons changed my mind. He got word to Matt by the prison grapevine that I was due out and that I had blood in my eye. So Matt talked Terry's mother into marryin' him. She was teachin' school at Bannack and Matt was handsome in them days and had a slick way with women."

When Jim Benton made no comment, Chiz continued. "The night I was due to show up at the ranch, Matt stayed in town on a big drunk, leavin' his wife alone at home. She had read the letter Ribs had sent Matt, but scared as she was, when I showed up, she asked me to put up my horse and stay to supper. We had a long talk. Matt had told her to smooth things over for him with me, but instead she told me she'd found out the mistake she had made in marryin' Matt, but she wouldn't quit him. When the Spiderweb declared war, Matt got shot to hell and I was crippled. Speck's father got killed and so the boy was kept at the ranch. When Terry's mother died, she made me promise to look after the kids. That's how come I stayed on. I couldn't whip a blind man, but I could look out for the two younguns," said Chiz quietly.

The two men rode the rest of the way in silence.

IX

The overcast in late afternoon was as gray as a dirty blanket, bringing down a cold drizzle like a dismal shroud.

As the two riders untied their saddle slickers, Old Chiz pointed a gloved finger between the ears of his horse. "Yonder's the Spiderweb Pass, that gun-notch dead ahead," he said, as they put on their slickers. "Half an hour from now you won't be able to make out the notch for the snow."

Jim Benton stared at the tight V-shaped notch in the sheer, almost perpendicular cliff walls hundreds of feet high on either side of the mountain. Beyond the sky was a slender column of daylight. From the ten-mile distance the notch had the deceptive look of not being wide enough for a man on horseback to ride through. Jim Benton mentioned this to Chiz.

"You're not far from wrong, Doc. There's a few places that will bother the Spiderweb longhorns. With a ten-foot spread between the horn tips, a few of the old mossyhorns will have to tilt their heads sideways, at that."

Jim Benton recalled the mounted head of the long-horned bull in the taproom. Even though he knew the longhorn breed of cattle were supposed to be immune to cattle ticks, he would hold them for inspection nevertheless.

"A horse can't turn around in the pass once you ride in," Old Chiz told him. "The ice and snow never melt in the narrows. The summer sun hits bottom for ten or fifteen minutes. No more."

Jim was willing to take the old cowpuncher's word for it. He had read where the wily Chief Joseph of the Nez Percés had almost succeeded in his attempt to trap Gibbons and his soldiers in his retreat north to Canada. The battle of the Little Big Horn had been fought within a few miles of the pass. And before that Lewis and Clark had marked it on their map. Outlaws on the dodge had put it to good use to check the pursuit of sheriffs' posses. It was an ideal gun trap.

"If Igo ain't trapped this side of the pass, Doc, don't be fool enough to follow him," advised Old Chiz. "You don't follow a mountain lion or a timber wolf into its cave."

Jim Benton agreed. His mind was busy going over and over snatches of rambling talk Cass had made through the black hours of delirium.

"There's the odd chance, Chiz," Jim Benton said, "that the trail boss will funnel the longhorns into the pass today sometime, instead of waiting until tomorrow morning."

"Funnel's the right word for it, Doc. That notch in the mountain is a five-mile bottleneck. Once the cattle are in, there's nowhere to go but out the other end. And you can gamble that Cass has got the best trail boss money can buy to ride point on that herd."

The cold drizzle had turned to icy sleet. Their slickers were stiff as sheet metal, and cold and clammy. Buttoned to the red flannel-lined collar, the shirts were flared out to cover the cantle and saddle skirts. Both riders wore leather shotgun chaps and short denim jackets under the slickers. But in spite of the protective clothing, both were cold to the marrow of their bones.

They were traveling light without a bed horse. And they could exist for a few days, if necessary, on the chunks of raw beef and salt they carried in their saddlebags.

The sleet had turned into hard dry snow,

and after a while the snow quit. As they climbed, the high mountain fog closed in before they were hardly aware of it. They saw it rolling down the mountainside, a gray avalanche of pea soup fog that brought with it an icy chill. Visibility was cut down to a scant hundred feet. Scrub pines were strangely distorted in height. It was like moving into a solid towering wall of gray that gave way for the horsebackers.

Jim Benton watched the ears of his horse prick forward. Chiz, riding ahead, reined up. Listening, they sat their horses.

They heard the distant sound of bawling cattle. For a brief moment the fog cleared and they saw the wedge-shaped opening into the pass. A good marksman could shoot a man as he sat his horse at the narrow entrance.

The horsebacker target was there now. There was no mistaking the tall Igo in a long black slicker and his high-crowned black hat, adding cubits to his stature as he stood up in his stirrups. The lean back made a tempting target. Both men had slid their saddle guns from the protective cover of their slickers. There was a wicked grin on Old Chiz's face as he shoved the rear sight to the last notch. He cut a look at his companion.

Jim Benton shook his head. "Igo's my meat, Chiz." He reined his horse behind boulders flanked by brush and scrub pines and motioned for Chiz to follow.

"We'll let the herd come through," he said. "A gun ruckus right now would gum the cards. The trail boss will be riding ahead of the lead steer, and no man in his right mind would ride out to get shot down."

"Lucky Igo didn't sight us first," Chiz said grimly. "The fog lifted just in time to give us the bulge. Igo don't shoot to miss."

Deciding they were safe, they waited for the longhorns to come out of the pass and head down the slope. They would scatter out of their own accord and graze on Spiderweb range. Igo would tally them through, then he'd probably head for the headquarters ranch to collect his money. And when the Spiderweb cowboys would go back through the pass to their trail outfit on the Idaho side of the mountain, Jim Benton and Old Chiz would step in.

"How long do you figure it'll take to get the cattle through?" Jim asked.

"It'll be dark," Chiz guessed.

Then they heard a high-pitched off-key chant:

Point 'em North,
To'rds the Promised Land,
And there's one more river to cross.
She's black as sin
Cold as death,
And there's one more river to cross.

They saw the singer. A man on a big palomino horse rode out from the pass. A long rawhide riata was dallied around his saddle horn, and at the end of the rope was a line-backed dun-colored steer, its twelve-foot spread of horns as black as the line down the steer's back.

"Old Rawhide," Chiz chuckled. "Tough as a boot. Fetched more cattle up the trail than any man alive."

The high-pitched chant knifed through the raucous din of the cattle that walk-bawled out of the pass. The rider on the palomino rode down the mountain trail, the longhorns following the lead steer. About a hundred yards down the slope the trail boss reined up, coiling his rope, until the trained lead steer came alongside. Reaching out, the rider slid the noose free of the horns.

The man rode back at a walk to Igo, sitting his horse. Neither man spoke as they sat their horses. Igo was counting five head at a time by spreading the fingers of one hand. He spoke the count aloud so that the trail boss could pick up the tally. To tally a hundred Igo tied a quick knot in one of his bridle reins.

The lowering temperature of approaching night made the fog a white blanket along the ground, until the whole mountainside was quilted. The grazing cattle and the two horsebackers were no longer visible, but the voices of the Spiderweb cowhands, moving with the cattle, filtered through the gray fog blanket.

"Wha' at is you, honey chile?" a cowhand called out.

"Down heah in de cawnfiel'! Los'!" came the answer.

As the dismal refrain caught on, others took it up, with added obscenities.

"You got the job done, old timer," Igo said to Rawhide. "Take your cotton pickers and get the hell back to Texas." Igo's ugly threat left its echo in the dead silence.

Through the fog came the trail boss's slow voice. "Igo's a hired killer with a gun in his hand, men," he told his cowhands when they rode up. There was no fear in his voice. "Don't give him any call to bust a cap. Let's get back to where the climate fits our henskin duds."

"I'm moving in on Igo," Jim Benton said. "Stay back out of sight where you can cover my back, Chiz."

"Have your gun in your hand, Doc," Old Chiz creaked, "and the hammer thumbed back. Igo's spoilin' for trouble."

The two men swung into their wet saddles.

"Lemme take the deal, Doc," Old Chiz whispered. "You're too young to die."

"Don't be shoving a lily in my hand. It's my job." Jim Benton rode off at a running walk. Old Chiz mounted and followed.

Old Rawhide and his trail hands headed into the pass. The sounds of shod hoofs and creaking saddle leather, the jingle of spur rowels and bit chains, were fitting music for the old trail boss's song as it echoed through the canyon walls.

For your hopes get cold,
  As the years get old,
And there's one more river to cross. . . .

Jim Benton and Old Chiz McDougal were two more shadowy horsebackers moving in the black night.

Taking off the wet glove on his right hand, Jim Benton flexed his cold fingers and rotated his hand to get the stiffness out of his wrists. He took his Colt .45 from the slicker pocket and laid it across the saddle behind the pommel.

He saw the blaze of the bonfire John Igo had made at the entrance of Spiderweb Pass. Igo, long legs spread apart, stood with his back to the blaze and peered into the pass. His hand was on the gun lever of the Winchester tucked under his right armpit.

The jumbled sounds from the pass blotted out the noise made by Jim Benton's horse as he rode up behind Igo. Picking up his six-shooter, Jim Benton thumbed back the hammer and lifted the gun until it was pointed at the killer's long back. The temptation to squeeze the trigger was strong, but shooting at a man's back, even to cripple him, was degrading to Jim Benton, and the temptation to fire died a-borning.

Keeping his thumb on the hammer, ready to fire if Igo happened to sight him, Jim let the gun hammer down and held the barrel tilted upward. Then he stiffened, tense as a coiled spring. Behind him and to the left a dry stick snapped and a bootheel scraped on a rock. The betraying crackle of a saddle slicker made Jim shiver. He was a plain target.

John Igo had heard the sounds. In a smooth unbroken movement he slid his carbine in a flat arc to follow the direction of the sound. From another angle came a chuckle. Igo stepped back cautiously to put him into the shadows.

"Stand tracked, Igo!" The saw-file voice belonged to Skeeter Owens. "Or you'll back into a knife point. Cass will be here directly. He sent me ahead to keep an eye on you." There was a deadly threat in the dry chuckle.

"What the hell kind of a trick are you tryin' to pull, Skeeter?" Igo shifted a little on his long legs.

"I got orders to keep you pinned down till the big boss gets here. Ooze into the firelight, Igo."

Reluctantly the killer moved toward the blazing logs. "You drunk, you short-complected little weasel?" Igo turned his head in the direction of Skeeter's voice.

"Wisht I was, you long-geared snake." Skeeter exchanged the compliment.

Keeping the carbine pointed in the direction of the voice, Igo slid a bottle from his slicker pocket. He thumbed the cork into his lean cheek and then took a dozen swallows before he lowered the bottle. He spat the cork into his hand and thumbed it into the bottle neck.

Shoving the bottle back into the deep pocket, he said, "Corn likker. Sets your guts afire." He backed closer to the blaze. "Those longhorns tallied out an even two thousand head. I get five bucks a head. Cass McCandless said he'd send the money by you, Skeeter." Igo showed his teeth. "He was stayin' at the ranch to have an alibi in case I had to do any killin'. You got the ten thousand on you, Skeeter? You got it made to kill me and go to the Hole with the money?" Igo seemed to be figuring things out. "I had it half way figured," Igo continued without raising his voice, "that there might be a cross up. That's why my Stock Inspector's clearance papers aren't signed. You kill me and the longhorns and the three other herds comin' in will go into quarantine. I'll get word to Jim Benton." Igo, his eyes reflecting the red glow of the fire, stood ramrod stiff. "You're not scarin' me a damned bit, you little knife-slingin' son of a bitch. Step into sight with that money Cass sent me."

"I done told you Cass is on the way, Igo," Skeeter said peevishly. "He sent me on ahead and said he'd be here as fast as he could make it."

"What slowed him up?" Igo asked suspiciously. "Somethin' go wrong?"

"He'll tell you when he gets here. And I hope it won't be too long. The seat of my britches is froze to the saddle," Skeeter complained. "Damn slicker's froze stiff as a board. And you bellied up to the fire with a bottle, bellyachin'."

"You got ten thousand dollars on you that belongs to me, Skeeter," Igo said in a deadly voice. "I've killed men for a hell of a lot less."

"Don't crowd your luck, Igo," Skeeter told him from behind chattering teeth. "That fire and a bottle of likker is worth killin' you for." He sounded as if he meant it.

"Then fetch me the money and thaw out. I might even spare you a drink. Once I get my money, I'm on my way. It's a long ride to Lost Trail Pass where I tally out the next Spiderweb cattle."

Skeeter was silent for a while. Then he said, "There's no percentage in me freezin' to death while I'm ridin' herd on you while you're huggin' a warm fire and a bottle."

Limping as he walked, the shriveled-up little man in a wet, yellow saddle slicker that trailed in the mud, stepped from behind the brush. Rain dripped from the low-pulled brim of his hat. As he came within reach, Igo held out the bottle. "Drink hearty, Skeeter." Igo grinned.

Skeeter had the neck of the bottle between his chattering teeth when the tall man spoke again. "Let's have the money." The barrel of the carbine in Igo's hand poked into the short man's slicker, ripping the stiff oilskin.

In a split second the half-emptied bottle jerked up with a swift movement and smashed into the cadaverous face of the killer. The wiry little Skeeter spun like a whirling dervish as the Winchester exploded. At the same instant a six-inch steel blade shot out from the switch-blade knife concealed in the sleeve of the little cowhand's slicker. It slashed across the back of Igo's gun hand, bone deep above the big knuckles. Igo let out a howl of pain. The carbine slid into the mud.

Skeeter staggered backwards, tripped and tried to regain his balance, but the bullet from Igo's carbine had hit. Skeeter, mortally wounded, sat in the mud. Bent over, he held his hands over his belly.

Igo backed away slowly, as blood trickled down his face from the cut on his fore-head. His good hand tore away his slicker and he reached for his six-shooter in a tied-down holster on his thigh.

There was no time for Jim Benton to think. He spurred his horse into the firelight as he all but rode down the Stock Inspector.

"One move for that gun, Igo, and I'll blow your skull open." Jim Benton gritted the warning.

Like a jack-knife Igo straightened up. He had been unaware of the horsebacker's approach. Empty-handed, his lipless mouth spread in a wolfish grin, he said, "You red-muzzled son of a bitch. I told you to quit the country. What the hell you doin' here?"

"I'm here to take you back to Bannack, to hang for the murder of Hank Sanford and for what you did to Judge Bryan."

Igo's reptilian eyes glittered. His grin was ghastly. Blood oozed between the fingers clamped across the back of his knife-cut hand. "I came back to Montana to clean my slate." His voice was menacing. "I shot that damned gossipin' stage driver because he was a Vigilante. I gave the Hanging Judge of Bannack a dose of his own medicine. And I gave you the same warning your father handed me, because your old man saved me from hangin'." The killer seemed to like the sound of his own voice. The murderous eyes flicked a contemptuous glance at the gun Benton pointed his way.

"I'm drunk, Benton," he said. "When I'm drunk, nothing this side of hell can stop me. I got knife-scratched, but that little weasel is gut shot. He'll be dead by the time I get you killed off. Too bad you didn't take that warning to quit Montana."

Igo's long arm snaked out. The bloody hand slapped the gun from Jim Benton's hand and his good hand grabbed the front of Jim's slicker. Something in Igo's eyes and in his tense posture warned Jim Benton.

Jim sat his saddle sideways, his feet braced in the stirrups and his hard-muscled legs tensed, ready for the yank on the front of his slicker. His legs were cantilever springs that shot him forward. His boots cleared the stirrups and as the horse jumped forward, Jim dropped down on the killer like a rodeo contestant bulldogging a steer. Igo reeled backwards and the two men went down in a snarled tangle. Igo's stinking whisky breath spewed in his face. His long fingers clawed at Jim Benton's eyeballs, then hooked in the corner of his mouth. Jim felt as if his face was being torn apart.

Jim Benton freed one hand, cocked it back in a balled fist and cracked it into the bony face, but the man's fingers clawed deeper. Jim released his grip on the skinny neck as he fought free and onto his feet. Half-blinded from the murderous gouging, he saw Igo as a long black shadow weaving drunkenly on long legs. Shaking his head to clear the pain, he saw Igo reach for his gun. In a prize fighter's crouch, Jim moved in fast with short, vicious punches that carried all his rawboned weight behind each blow. He doubled Igo up with a low blow, and as the man's head raised, he snapped it back with a savage uppercut to the jaw. Then he threw his Sunday punch, a haymaker that stretched Igo out on his back in the mud. He looked dead enough to bury.

Jim Benton's face was an ugly smear of mud and oozing blood. Pain shot through his eyeballs. His knees trembled, but he had whipped his man. During the fight Igo had used his long legs to advantage by kneeing and kicking. The pain was dulled by the heat of combat, but now it was catching up.

He wondered if he had killed Igo. Not that it mattered, one way or the other. Standing on unsteady legs, he was but vaguely aware of shod hoofs sloshing through the mud.

"You're a sorry-looking son of a bitch, Benton." Cass McCandless' voice jerked Jim's head up. The big cowman's laugh was like the bawling roar of a mad bull.

Cass sat his horse not a dozen feet away. His gun was pointed at Jim Benton's belly. Despite the weather and his recent illness, the big man wore only a double-breasted red flannel shirt with large white mother-of-pearl buttons. The grin, as he looked down on Jim Benton, was as cold as winter ice. Leaning a little forward against the saddle horn, he motioned to the man on the ground. "Dead?" he growled.

Jim Benton spat out some blood. "Igo's on ice," he said. "I'm taking him to Bannack for hanging."

Paying no attention to McCandless' gun, Jim Benton removed the torn slicker. He wondered where Old Chiz McDougal was.

"You're taking nobody no place." Cass bared his teeth in a snarl. "Get a gun in your hand, Benton."

Jim Benton wiped the mud and blood from his face with his wet shirt tail, then tucked it into his Levi's. He looked up at the big man on horseback.

"Step down, McCandless," he said with a contemptuous twist in his challenge. "I lost my gun. I'll fight you for yours."

A bull-like roar tore from Cass' massive chest. He swung down and stood there for a second. Lowering his head, he charged, using the gun as a club as he chopped at the other man's bared head.

Jim Benton had anticipated the blind, bull rush and jumped sideways before the gun barrel chopped down with a wild swing. As the big man, carried by his own momentum, rushed past, Jim Benton swung at the heavy jaw. McCandless dropped like a beef hit with a sledge hammer. Jim grabbed the gun from his limp hand.

At a sound made by the little knife man, Jim swung around, surprised to see him still alive. "I had you checked off the list, Skeeter," he said.

"I hung and rattled while you and Igo fought it out. I was fixin' to gut shoot Igo if he came out on top," Skeeter said. "Then when McCandless rode up, I let you cold-cock him. That's the first time any son of a bitch ever knocked out Cass McCandless. I'll whittle you a leather medal, Benton."

Jim Benton, rubbing the skinned knuckles of his hand, watched Old Chiz ride into the firelight.

"A day late and a dollar short. That's me

all over," Old Chiz said, as he stepped from his saddle and stood close to the fire.

Cass groaned and opened his eyes. Rolling over on all fours, he got slowly to his feet. He picked up his hat, slapped the dirt off and yanked it down on his head. There was a forced grin on his mud-splattered face as he looked at his gun in Jim Benton's hand.

"Whipped me and took my gun," he said. "By God, that's one for the book."

"You're still a sick man, McCandless. That fever took a lot out of you. You were a pushover."

"Like hell," Cass retorted. He walked over to Skeeter, who sat hunched over. "What the hell's wrong with you? You so drunk you can't stand up?"

Raw hate glinted in the little man's beady eyes. Slowly he pulled back the front of his slicker so that Cass could get a look at his bloodstained shirt and Levi's.

"Who shot you?" Cass blurted. "Benton?"

"Igo." Skeeter spat the name out like a dirty word. "The bastard you pinned a Stock Inspector's tin badge on." He pulled the slicker together.

With the swiftness of a black lizard's tongue a switchblade knife slid from Skeeter's slicker sleeve. As he held the deadly weapon palmed in his hand, a ghastly grin spread on the wizened face.

"You sent me on ahead, Cass," the words came through clenched teeth, "to hold Igo till you got here. He figured I had his payoff money in my pocket."

The big man shifted his weight uneasily. He narrowed his eyes at the wounded man. "What did you tell him?"

"Not what you think, Cass." The thin lips twisted. "I didn't tell Igo that the best he'd get would be a Mexican standoff from the cattle king of the Panhandle when he showed up." Skeeter's dry chuckle rattled in his tight throat. He held the knife balanced in his hand.

Cass' florid face looked mottled in the firelight. A wicked grin crossed the leathery face of the wounded man. "When we rode up on the lead steer, Cass," Skeeter's voice had a dead tone, "you knew your longhorns had come through and you sent me on ahead to make your standoff dicker with the Stock Inspector." A short laugh tore from his insides. "I was damn fool enough to let Igo sucker me in with a bottle of rotgut. Drink hearty, he says, and gut shot me as I took the first swallow. He was fixin' to get that ten thousand I didn't have when Benton rode up and took the deal." Skeeter pointed with his knife.

"Yonder goes your convict water moccasin," he croaked, "snakin' through the mud. Give Cass his gun, Benton, and we'll see how he makes out with his Mexican standoff."

Jim Benton put the gun into Cass' hand. "Have at it, big mister," he said. He had picked up his own gun and had cleaned it while Skeeter and Cass were talking.

John Igo had managed to crawl crabwise away from the revealing glow of the campfire. He got to his feet and sidled furtively behind his high-withered horse. His maimed hand wrapped in a handkerchief, he kept it raised above the neck of his horse and hooked his elbow around the steel horn. He had his Colt gun laid across the saddle to hold it steady. Only his bared head, his coarse black hair plastered down by the rain, and his shoulders showed. His eyes were splinters of hate set in a horrible mask of blood and mud.

The bandaged hand waved back and forth like a treacherous white flag of truce. The gun, swinging to and fro in a flat arc, covered the three men at the campfire.

"I got ten thousand dollars comin',

McCandless." The raw wind whipped the words from Igo's lipless mouth. "Pay off or die."

Jim Benton cut a sidelong glance at the big cowman. Cass, his boots spur deep in mud, stood tracked. His thumbs were hooked into the cartridge belt around his belly. His hand was within quick reach of his gun.

"Talk fast, Cass." Skeeter's chuckle rattled, as he held the knife ready to throw.

The big cowman was no longer swaying on widespread legs. Cass McCandless had sobered up. There was no fear showing as he faced the lanky killer.

"Kill me, Igo," he barked out, "and you stand to lose fifty thousand dollars. You'll get paid when the rest of the cattle are inspected and passed, and you've signed the clearance papers."

"Ten thousand laid on the line right now," Igo rasped. "Another thousand bounty money when I shoot Benton."

Cass McCandless hesitated as if he were deciding something. "How much, Benton, do you calculate offhand it would cost to impound ten thousand head of Spiderweb cattle and dip them at the government vats?"

"Not over five thousand dollars," Jim

Benton replied without taking his fixed stare from Igo and his gun.

"That throws your tin badge and your price of fifty thousand into the discard, Igo!" Cass let out a bellowing laugh.

Jim Benton saw Igo's gun barrel move. The snarl that came from the killer was like the howl of a timber wolf. Jim threw himself flat as Igo's gun jetted flame. He heard the blast of McCandless' six-shooter. Then he saw Igo in the saddle, his lanky torso bent across the saddle horn, as he made his getaway.

As Jim Benton cocked his gun for a shot at Igo, a woman screamed. "Here's your payoff, Igo!" she cried, and then the crack of a .38. The scream was blotted out as suddenly as it had come.

Old Chiz spurred past and was swallowed up in the black maw of the night. Jim Benton, his gun in his hand, scrambled to his feet. Cass McCandless, swaying drunkenly, lurched and fell forward. Shot through the heart, he was dead when he struck the ground.

Jim Benton ran crouched over. He almost stumbled over Alison McCandless, who lay in a motionless heap just beyond the outer rim of the fire. She was dead. Jim covered her with what was left of his slicker.

Two horsebackers took shape as they rode out of the fog. They were Chiz McDougal and the Spiderweb trail boss. Rawhide had the dead body of John Igo dragging at the end of his long riata. Igo had lived long enough to stretch rope.

When there was no comment from Skeeter Owens, Jim Benton went over to investigate. Skeeter was dead.

"Alison's dead, Chiz," Jim told him. "I wonder why she didn't go to Bannack as she promised me she'd do?"

"While me'n' her was behind the rocks watchin' the whole show in the fire light, she told me she had promised herself to be around to shoot Igo, if he tried to get away.

She called out to him as he passed us, but bein' faster on the draw, he shot her just as she pulled the trigger of her .38."

"I should have made you take her back to Bannack, Chiz."

"No use blamin' yourself, Doc. Alison had it made."

Chiz reached into his pocket and handed Jim a chamois bag. "Alison said to give you this," Chiz said. "Inside is twenty-five thousand dollars. You're to use the money to pay your way through medical school."

Jim Benton took the bag and put it into

236

his pocket. There was nothing he could say. The trail boss had dismounted and was standing with his back to the fire. Jim walked over to talk with him.

"After Igo run me and my boys through Spiderweb Pass, I left the men at camp and rode back. I come back to collect six months' wages the Spiderweb owed us," Rawhide said gruffly. "When Igo was makin' his getaway, he took a shot at me, so I roped him around the neck and dragged him from the saddle."

Jim listened quietly to the old trail boss. "You're ramrodding the Spiderweb from here on, Rawhide," Jim told him. "I'll hold you responsible to hold the four trail herds in quarantine until I can get in new supplies and set up new dipping vats. I'll send some Nester Pool men out to help you."

Jim Benton took the money from the chamois bag and handed it to Rawhide. "Pay yourself and your men with this Spiderweb money," he said. "And send a couple of your trail hands to the ranch headquarters to fetch a spring wagon to take Alison McCandless' body to Bannack. The roundup wagon will do for the others."

While Jim Benton and Old Chiz McDougal kept vigil over the dead girl, a cold dawn swept the last wisps of gray fog across the campfire. Jim took the will, which Alison had made out, from Cass McCandless' pocket. "Here goes the Spiderweb, Chiz," he said, as he tossed the paper into the blaze. "But I'll do what I can to see that those nester cowmen get back their outfits when the Spiderweb ranch comes up for Sheriff's sale."

From down below came the rattle of wheels, as the spring wagon and the bed wagon came into view.

"We should make Bannack by sundown, Doc," Old Chiz said. The eyes of the two men met and held. Both were sharing the same thought.

"A hot bath and the works at the barber shop, Doc," Chiz said. "We'll slough off what's behind us when we wash off this muck that's on us. Ain't every day a man gets a chance to give a bride away."

"If she'll have me," Jim Benton said quietly. "I've got a couple of things to talk over with Terry first."

"Keep your mouth shut, Doc," Old Chiz snorted. "I've raised Terry and I know her better than you do. There's no percentage in hurtin' her about something she's too young to savvy." Old Chiz indicated with his head the covered body of Alison

McCandless.

Both men were silent for a while. Then Chiz pulled the cork on his bottle and said in a waspish voice, "You want for us to drink together? Or should I bend this bottle across your bonehead?" Jim took the bottle and drank.

Tonight, Jim Benton was thinking, when they reached Bannack, he and Terry Wagner would be married by Judge Bryan. Tomorrow Alison McCandless would be given a Christian burial. Then he'd pick up his government job where he had left off.

Alison had failed to take word to the nester cowmen to guard the passes, which was just as well, because now it wouldn't be necessary. But he would ask Bill Irvin and the others to help with the dipping of the Texas cattle. After that was done, he would think about the future.

Jim Benton shrugged his shoulders as he thought about the money Alison had given him for medical school. What if he had tossed it back into the Spiderweb, he had cured a man stricken with the deadly Rocky Mountain Spotted Fever. He had proven the theory of Dr. Roscoe Spencer that the cattle tick caused the same deadly fever in human beings.

He'd take his full report to Dr. Spencer

and return to the practice of veterinary medicine. When he'd saved enough money, he would go through medical school. Six years from now he would hang out his shingle in Bannack:

JAMES BENTON, M.D.